Contents

Get Free Books

Do you love western romance with a little suspense? Join Lynn's monthly newsletter to stay updated on what's happening in my world and get a free copy of

"A Question of the Heart," *the first installment of the Questioning Hearts Series.*

Can the blacksmith win the heart of the town baker?

Chapter 1

Psalms 147:3
He heals the brokenhearted and binds up their wounds.

Heavy footsteps vibrate the pine floor of the one-bedroom room rental in the boarding house. "Open the door, woman!" Saul curses, stumbling, and fumbling as he pounds on the door, screaming.

Anika whispers to Delaney, "Hide, Angel. Don't come out unless I call you." Delaney runs and cowers in the corner behind the chair. Anika smooths her shirt over her swollen belly and walks to the door. "Coming, Saul," she opens the door, and a sudden slap sends her stumbling backward into a table.

"What the hell took you so long? You gettin' so fat with child that you can't even walk?" Saul laughs at his own joke as she wipes the blood from her split lip. Anika straightens up and slowly closes the door. Saul Coltrane stands five feet eleven inches tall, just five inches taller than her, but he is all muscle. Once, her husband was good-looking, but now his cheeks are sunken and yellow. His beard is long and unkempt, as is his hair. The biggest change is his eyes. Any affection he once held for her is gone, replaced with simmering hatred.

"I'm sorry, Saul," Anika whimpers, covering her

pregnant belly. The baby isn't due for another four months. "I- I kept your dinner warm for you." She moves to the small woodstove in the corner and pulls a plate of food from it. After placing it on the small table, she backs away, careful to avoid eye contact.

"Good, I'm starving." He stomps to the table and sits, stuffing down the potatoes and a piece of meat she managed to get during dinner. Food goes quickly in the boarding house. It is served promptly at seven pm, and if you aren't early, it goes fast. Anika helps prepare the meals, and they give her a discount on food.

Anika stares at him with caramel-colored eyes and pushes her strawberry blonde hair back. Her face is swelling quickly; she winces when she licks her lip. Saul wasn't always abusive. Before the war, her husband was kind and loving, but after, he couldn't stay in one place very long. He was quick to anger and drank to help ease the pain. Nightmares plagued him, and the easy access to cheap whiskey became his solution. The latest move brought them to Pennsylvania six months ago, where he started working at the mill.

The first time he hit her, she was shocked. With no family to turn to, Anika was alone, except for their daughter, seven-year-old Delaney. After the first time, his rage seemed to grow. Everything seemed to set him off, and Anika began to wonder how long she would survive. They moved from town to town before settling here, and the church became her refuge. Drinking became his medicine to numb the pain of whatever ate at his soul. The one saving grace was that he never hit Delaney. He has a soft spot for his daughter, and Anika hopes for this child as well.

"Did you make any money today?" Saul demands

not even bothering to look at her. Rising from his chair, he moves to the small table where he keeps his whiskey and pours another cup.

"Yes. I made a dollar fifty, doing laundry." It was a good sum; the men and women who board often used the laundry services. Saul grunts and glares at her.

"Well, where is it?" The bottle is drained dry as he drinks the last of it before swaying on his feet and stumbling towards her.

"We were behind on the rent, Saul. They kept the money for this week's payment and said if we can't pay on time..." The blow to her face sends her sprawling on the floor. Anika grunts and tries to cover her belly.

"You, stupid pig," he starts kicking her, grunting with each word. Pain explodes in her side and stomach. Anika can't catch her breath as the blows drive it from her.

"No, the baby..." Anika screams. Her only thought is to protect herself and keep his focus on her, not Delaney. Fighting for survival now, she grabs his pant leg, causing him to stumble backward into the small table and chair.

"I'll kill you!!" He roars, stumbling to his feet.

"No, Daddy!" Delaney screams, flinging herself on top of her mother. Saul steps back and stares down at them. Anika groans as she tries to sit up, but the pain in her back and stomach is ripping around her midsection.

Saul stumbles backward and trips over the chair, then kicks the table across the room. Flinging open the door, he runs from the boarding house towards Schmidt Bar and Saloon, the local drinking hall. Anika feels her water break and begins to pant hard as the first contraction hits.

"Mommy," Delaney sobs out.

"I'm alright, Angel. I need you to be strong now. Go get Mrs. Daniels, tell her the baby is coming. I need Dr. Parker." Delaney scrubs her face and nods.

"Yes, Mama," she runs from the room crying and yelling for Mrs. Daniels.

The next few hours pass in a blur as the Doctor comes with his wife, and her daughter is born. Anika holds her in her arms and sobs as she draws her first and only breath in this life. "Nooo..." she moans, rocking her. "I'm so sorry."

Dr. Parker wipes a tear and looks up at his wife. Josiah and Clara Parker have patched her up more times than she cares to think about, and right now, they are at a loss for words. "This isn't your fault, Anika. I can give you some morphine for pain," Dr. Parker offers, but she immediately shakes her head.

"No, Delaney needs me. Where is she?" Anika glances around the room in a panic.

"Easy, now. Mrs. Daniels has her, and we are going to take her home with us, so you can rest," Clara insists.

Anika looks up, and her tears roll down her swollen bruised cheek. "Thank you, I think that would be a blessing." Her eyes look down at the tiny bundle who has entered the world too early and presses one last kiss to her little face.

"She's beautiful, isn't she?"

"Perfection," Clara replies softly.

"Are you ready?" Josiah says a prayer asking for guidance and waits for her to hand the child to him. He knows the longer she waits, the harder it will be to let go.

Trembling arms hold up the newborn, and Anika moans a heartbroken sound as he takes her gently into his arms. "Would you like to name her before we go?"

"Her name is... Rosie Coltrane," Anika whispers and wipes her eyes.

"Rosie is a beautiful name." Clara sits with her and hugs Anika while her husband leaves the room quickly. When he returns a half hour later, he brings a dropper of morphine.

"Anika, Mrs. Daniels is going to stay with you tonight, and we are taking care of Delaney. I insist you let me give you something for the pain." Anika looks up at him and laughs a sound bordering on hysteria.

"Will it heal the chasm in my soul, Dr. Parker?" No more tears fall. She is cried out for the moment. "Tomorrow I must tell my daughter that her sister is dead, and I can't promise that we won't be next. Thank you, but no thank you. If he comes back, I... I have to be ready."

Josiah is livid. He has already spoken with the Sheriff, and he is out looking for Saul. Something has to be done to help these wounded soldiers. Too many women and children are paying the price. With all the men coming home from the war, saloons are on the rise. The church is trying to counsel families and push for change. In the meantime, they do what they can. He reaches over and pats her hand.

"You won't be alone this time. The Sheriff is going to put him in lockup for a little while to help get his head straight. We've already spoken with the Pastor, and they are going to help you and Delaney. I don't want you to be afraid tonight. Just rest and let your body heal. I think you have a few cracked or bruised ribs. Unfortunately, that could take a few weeks for the black and blue bruising to fade and heal. I don't see any reason why you can't have more children in the future. Please reconsider the drops for pain. You will heal quicker if you rest."

"All right then, just this once." Dr. Parker sighs with relief and quickly gives her the morphine before she changes her mind. "Thank you," Anika's eyes are already closing as true exhaustion hits her. They file out slowly, and Mrs. Daniels promises to call if the bleeding gets worse or her pain increases.

Clara waits with Josiah while Mrs. Daniels goes to get Delaney and hugs her husband tightly. "Josiah," she whimpers.

"I know, my love. We're going to pray hard and find a way to help them." Delaney comes quietly down the hallway and stares up at them with her beautiful hazel eyes.

"Is my Mama dead?" She asks suddenly.

Clara gasps and squats down immediately. "No Delaney, your Mother is sleeping. Dr. Parker took really good care of her. We would like to take you home with us for the night though, so she can heal and sleep. Is that okay with you?" Delaney stares hard at her and glances at the door, chewing on her lip. Each time her mother is hurt, they let her stay with them.

"Okay, can Buddy sleep with me?" She asks hopefully thinking about their dog.

"Buddy wouldn't sleep with anyone else," Clara laughs and takes her hand, leading her to the carriage outside. "Let's go see him."

Chapter 2

Anika wakes to whispers and footsteps, but she can't seem to force herself to open her eyes just yet. "What do we tell her?" Mrs. Daniels whispers.

"Is it too soon?" Another voice asks.

"The poor lass won't be able to bear it," a third voice says a little louder. Anika's heart begins to pound as she thinks immediately of Delaney. Adrenaline rushes through her body, and she jerks straight up in bed and stares at the three women.

"What's wrong? Is it Delaney?" She demands through her swollen, split lip.

All three women jump, and Mrs. Daniels gasps, "Merciful heavens!" She rushes to prop a pillow up behind Anika and reassures her. "No, Delaney is fine; she is with Dr. Parker and Clara."

A cup of water is pressed into her hand, and someone hands her a fresh damp cloth for her face. Anika drinks it gratefully and washes her face and neck before running out of patience.

"Mrs. Daniels, I can't thank you enough for all you've done for me, but you said you needed to tell me something."

The other two ladies immediately excuse

themselves, grabbing linens to wash and swiftly leave, promising to return later. Mrs. Daniels sits heavily on the side of the bed, patting her silver hair. Ever so gently, she takes Anika's hand.

"Sweets, you need to steel yourself. Be strong for Delaney," taking a deep breath, she spills it as quickly as she can. "Your husband was shot and killed last night at the saloon."

Anika stares at her as all the color fades from her face, making the bruises stand out even more shockingly. She falls back onto her pillows and presses a fist to her mouth, closing her eyes.

"Be strong, Mrs. Coltrane," Mrs. Daniels pleads, hugging her tightly and soothing her as Anika struggles to contain her reaction.

"How?" She manages to choke out. Tremors roll over her body as she listens to the story.

"He was drunk on whiskey and lager, you see; he accused someone of cheating at cards. A fight started, and they shot him dead in the ruckus."

"I see." Dead, he's never going to hit her again, she thinks. We are free, her heart screams. "I... thank you for telling me. If you don't mind, could I have some time... alone?" Anika asks quietly.

"Of course, I will have some breakfast brought to you. Just rest now." She watches the poor woman rush from the room, barely holding back her laughter. Anika laughs until her tears turn to sobs.

"God forgive me," she cries. Relief rushes through her body as she thinks about her freedom. All cried out, she sleeps until the sun is setting and manages to get up and start walking.

What sound does a heart make when it breaks? As

she slowly cleanses her body and changes into a gown, the sight of her empty belly causes her to double over in agony. Anika wonders how it is possible that the world does not hear the screams of her soul. Slow, deep breaths, and she stands back up to finish dressing. Her breasts are full. Within a few days, the first of her milk will come in. She tries not to think of her sweet angel. Dinner is broth and bread, and she forces herself to eat, grateful to have the nourishment. Delaney will need her to be strong.

"I have to bury my husband and my daughter, then figure out what I'm going to do."

Delaney leaps from the carriage the next morning and rushes into the boarding house as fast as her little legs will carry her. Bursting into the room, she stops and stares at her mother in the rocking chair. "Delaney," Anika calls and opens her arms as she rushes to her.

Piercing hazel eyes travel over her mother's bruised and battered face and land on her stomach. Tears glisten, as she glances around the room, "Mama?" She pleads. It is a plea of denial, but Anika can only give her the truth.

"It's going to be alright, Delaney. We need to talk." Delaney runs forward and drops to her knees, putting her head in her mama's lap.

"No, Mama," she whimpers as Anika strokes her head.

"As long as we have each other, everything else will work out." Together they cry, and when she tells her of her sister, more tears follow.

Chapter 3

Four days later, dressed in a borrowed black dress from Clara, Anika smooths her skirt over her swollen waist. She took careful time to look nice this morning, allowing her strawberry curls loose around her shoulders and pulled up on the sides. It was her way of rebelling against Saul one last time. He hated when she did her hair and threatened to cut it off the last time she didn't pull it straight back into a tight bun. Glancing at her, you would almost not know that she had lost a baby just a few days earlier. Weight gain was not a problem with money scarce during her pregnancy and her body was quickly recovering.

They ride with the doctor and his wife to the gravesite, and Anika blocks out the voices around her. The warm August air blows across her, but even the morning sun can't warm her soul. Delaney holds tightly to her hand and she can't help but think about the future. Now when she envisions it, there is no pain or fear only hope that things will get better, so she can give Delaney a better life. As the caskets are lowered into the ground inside the cemetery outside of town, the pastor's voice pulls her to the present.

"The bible says, 'Blessed are those who mourn, for

they shall be comforted.' Seek first the word of God and understanding will follow. Thank you for coming." The pastors seize the opportunity for a quick sermon on serving our neighbors before he concludes. Thankfully, the church paid for the funerals. A few members from the boarding house came, all had kind words of encouragement and sympathy, but Anika is relieved to see them leave. After the last person leaves, she asks to speak to the Pastor privately. Clara leads Delaney to the wagon as her husband waits nearby.

"Mrs. Coltrane, if there is anything I can do for you and Delaney just say the word." Pastor Donegal is Irish with a brogue that makes her smile. Standing next to the fresh mounds of dirt, staring at the tombstones Anika can't bring herself to look at him.

"I think we should pray for my soul, Pastor. I'm so full of hatred towards him. Does that mean I'm evil?"

"Evil?" He looks at her face swollen and bruised before he speaks. "No, Mrs. Coltrane. Human? Yes. You lost a child you loved, from the man who was supposed to protect and honor you. Hatred is a normal feeling, but you must not let it taint your soul. In time you should seek to forgive him, for the demons that rode his soul were many."

"Forgive him?" Anika looks at him in surprise. "How, if I can't forgive myself. If I were stronger..."

"Nay," he takes her hands in his and squeezes gently. "From what I have heard you protected Delaney and honored your husband. It is impossible to forget what has transpired, you lost a child and a husband. If it were easy to forgive, we would simply remove it from our memories. The first step is accepting that God is in control. He commands us to forgive and forget, in our faith, we must obey our Father."

Anika stares past him to her daughter staring solemnly back at her. "I want to, but I'm not sure how to do that."

"That's easy, seek him first. Pray, and love your daughter. Feel the anger, but don't let it take root in your soul or it will blot out all the love you have. If that happens you will isolate Delaney and leave her alone in this world." Pastor Donegal watches his words sink in. "She needs you now to guide her, can you try to do that?"

Anika wipes a stray tear and nods her head. "I will try," she whispers.

"That's all I ask." He pats her shoulder and walks away giving her a moment of privacy.

Dropping to her knees on the ground, she places a flower on Rosie's mound of dirt. "Father, hold her close in your loving embrace." Delaney runs to her mother and gently lays a flower beside hers. Anika takes her hand and pulls her to the ground next to her. "Pray with me Delaney," she pleads, and she bows her little head and listens.

"Father, help us to understand that you are in control and trust in your plan for our lives. We give ourselves completely to you. Guide us, protect us, and help us to forgive him." Delaney stiffens beside her and tries to pull away, but Anika will not budge. "I will not let hatred plant a seed in our souls. Today we are free in our love for you and each other, knowing that your son paid the ultimate price to wash away our sins." Turning to Delaney she clasps her face in her hands, "Only God is perfect, Delaney."

"I hate Daddy, Mama!" Hazel eyes glare at her and she smiles at her daughter.

"It is okay to hate what he did to us and our family, but not the man. He was good once, Delaney. He was sick and lost... and now he is home. We will cry together, be angry together and then you know what?"

"What?" She whispers with tears running down her cheeks.

"We will heal together, I promise." Delaney throws her arms around her neck and sobs.

Pastor Donegal watches with Mr. and Mrs. Parker and smiles softly. "God is good; it may not feel like it today, but we must trust in His plan." Guilt rides all the members of the church on this day. The law did fail to protect them, and the church tried to counsel him many times, but war stains a soul. If one does not have a strong faith, it is hard to survive the scars. He nods goodbye and returns to his wagon.

Clara wipes a tear as she watches Mother and child. She turns to look at her husband, "We have to help them." He nods in silent agreement, turning at the sound of a horse riding fast in their direction, and a familiar voice calls out for help.

"Dr. Parker, we need your help." The rider pulls up short but doesn't bother to dismount. "It's Sue Ward; she's taken a turn for the worse."

Josiah glances worriedly at his wife. Anika and Delaney rode with them in their wagon, and he can't abandon them. Unfortunately, it isn't safe for the women to travel back to town alone. Sue Ward lives in Mt. Joy ten miles outside of town, and that is a fast ride on horseback. In the wagon, it will take longer.

Clara rushes to explain, and Anika calls out, "We will go with you, Dr. Parker. It isn't a problem."

Relief rushes across his face, "Are you sure you can

handle the trip?" Anika and Delaney follow Clara's lead and quickly enter the wagon.

"I won't keep you from helping someone in need. You're my doctor; I will defer to your judgment." Josiah looks over the young woman's swollen face and decides to chance it. Sue may not have much time, and he wants to be there to help.

"Right then. Let's go." Climbing up next to his wife, he turns to the young man. "William, ride ahead and tell them I'm on my way." Will doesn't wait; he kicks the horse into a run, and they follow at a safe pace.

Josiah does his best to avoid the rough patches of the road as Clara explains the situation to Anika. "Glenn and Sue Ward own a farm in Mt. Joy, called Ward Farm and Orchards. She has always had a weak heart, but the stress of the war and pregnancy took a toll on her body. The twins were delivered two weeks ago."

"Did they?" Anika can't finish the sentence as she bounces along holding Delaney close.

"Yes, twins born a month early. Sue is not faring as well as the infants," Josiah responds.

"That's sad," Delaney murmurs, turning her face into her Mother's embrace.

"What can you do Josiah, to help her?" Clara asks her husband.

"In truth, I've done all I can do. Now it is a matter of treating the symptoms and trying to make her comfortable. Frankly, I'm surprised she has lived this long. It has been two weeks, but a mother's love makes one capable of amazing feats." He says thinking of Anika and Delaney.

Clara blinks back tears and murmurs a prayer for the Ward family. Anika bows her head and lifts a prayer for them as well. Everyone has a burden to bear she thinks pulling Delaney close for a hug.

The noon sun climbs high into the sky, and the beauty of it kissing the emerald landscape takes her breath. Anika stares in wonder at the lush rolling hills of the countryside around them. Her pain is beginning to beat at her as they bounce along. She closes her eyes and bites her lip as Josiah calls out to her.

"We're almost there, do you need to stop?"

"No, I'm fine." The wind blows, and she inhales deeply, drawing in the smell of fresh grass.

"Oh Mama, look at all the trees!" Delaney shouts, startling Anika.

"Delaney, those are apple trees. They are part of the Orchard," Clara explains. Soon they come to a turn and travel a few hundred feet down the lane and pass under a wooden sign. "Ward Farm and Orchards." In the distance at the end of the dusty road is a large two-story brick farmhouse. Two large dogs run alongside the wagon, barking, and leaping at them as Dr. Parker slows the wagon before stopping and leaps down. He rushes to the back of the wagon to grab his medical bag and turns to help his wife down.

"Dr. Parker, thank you for coming." An older woman with white hair nods to them and guides him inside as her husband snaps at the dogs and orders the stable hands to take care of the horses.

"Allow me to help you, ladies." Tall, muscular, and silver-haired, with skin aged from the sun and life, Allen Ward greets them with a warm smile. When he reaches out a hand, Delaney cowers back away from him and into her mother's side.

Clara puts a hand on his arm and smiles, "That's

very kind of you Allen, but I haven't gotten to hug this sweetheart all day." She adeptly steps in front of him and reaches out for Delaney, who instantly reaches for her.

Allen glances back at Anika with a small frown and notices the bruising and widow attire. "Allow me to introduce Mrs. Coltrane and her daughter Delaney Coltrane," Clara says making the introductions.

Anika takes his hand and is thankful for the help. When he grips her waist to lower her to the ground, she hisses and pales at the pain in her ribs. Swaying on her feet, he steadies her and waits for her to gather herself.

"Steady now," Allen murmurs.

"Thank you," she whispers, too ashamed to look him in the eye.

"Welcome to Ward Farm. Let's get you inside. How does a glass of juice fresh from our orchard sound?" Allen asks Delaney. Her hazel eyes light up, but she waits for her mother to speak.

Anika smiles softly. "That would be lovely." Pain is rippling down her back and legs from the trauma of the last few days. Tentatively, she follows them inside, thankful that he chatters and teases a smile from Delaney.

"Daisy will have my hide if I don't settle you in the parlor. Please have a seat." Allen glances worriedly at Anika. "Refreshments, coming up."

"Let me help, Allen," Clara offers, and they move into the kitchen. As soon as they are out of earshot, he glances at her with a question in his eyes.

"That woman has been sorely mistreated," he states. Clara doesn't bother denying the obvious.

"We were at the funeral for her husband and newborn daughter, Allen. The baby... came early and it was too soon." Protective of Anika's privacy she doesn't fill him in on the details, but he doesn't need her to. Only a blind man would miss the evidence of her face and movements.

"I'm sorry to call you away from that, have you had lunch yet?" He asks.

"Not yet, Allen, but don't concern yourself."

Allen is already calling to the housekeeper who comes instantly from the garden out behind the house. "Ms. Pearl, we will need luncheon served for four more, please."

"Of course, Mr. Ward." Pearl hurries to prepare lunch while Allen grabs a tray and glasses for the juice.

"Tell me, how are the boys?"

"They grow weaker every day," Allen replies hoarsely. "She can't feed them, and they reject every kind of milk we offer. I fear it is in God's hands now." He adds biscuits to the tray and they walk back to the living room.

Anika glances around the grand foyer and is instantly reminded of home. Born in Virginia, she grew up on a smaller version of this farm. From the heart of pine floors to the beautiful fireplace, she runs her hand over the mantle and sighs. Her parents died during an outbreak of smallpox. She was already married and a new mother when they passed. The pain in her body draws her from her memories and she is thankful for the moments of privacy to relax. The wagon ride didn't help her ribs, though walking seems to help. A noise filters in through the pain and causes her to frown.

"Mama, do you hear that?" Delaney stands up and moves towards a hallway. Meowing, like the sound of a kitten in pain. Anika turns slowly, ignoring the waves of exhaustion and follows the sound.

Her heart clenches at the familiar sound pulling her out of the sitting room and down a corridor. The cries grow stronger causing her feet to pick up pace. Delaney follows her, watching Anika stop outside of a door. It is cracked open and the cries have grown louder now. Trembling, she pushes open the door and watches as Daisy, Allen's wife, struggle to soothe twin infants.

"I'm sorry to disturb you," Anika says, "It's just that we heard the cries."

Daisy sighs and places the baby back in his bassinet. "That's alright. I'm Daisy Ward, Grandma to these tiny bundles." Daisy's hands are shaking, and she struggles to keep back tears as the baby whimpers and hiccups, finally sucking his fist.

"I'm Anika Coltrane, and this is my daughter Delaney."

Anika steps to the side of the wooden cradle and glances down. Two tiny dark-haired babies, frail and whining are sucking on tiny fists. "They're so small, Mama. Are they supposed to look like that?" Delaney whispers.

"No sweets, they were born early." Looking at them, Anika whispers, "So beautiful."

"My daughter-in-law, Sue can't nurse them. Her milk didn't come. They've lost more weight, unfortunately, and they are not responding to the cow's milk. We've tried every kind, but it only causes them pain," Daisy explains and smiles weakly behind them as her husband and Clara join them.

Another mewling cry calls out and Anika's body responds. Breasts heavy with milk and a heart laden with pain she glances down at Delaney when she takes her hand and asks, "Can't you help them, Mama?"

No one moves, and it seems as if time stops still for a moment. A single tear breaks free rolling down Anika's face, "Yes, I can," she whispers hoarsely.

Anika takes a deep breath and prays quietly in her heart before she makes the offer. Glancing at the shocked faces of those around her, she stiffens her spine and says, "What you need is a wet nurse."

Clara gasps, "No," and steps to her side. "No, it's too much to ask, Anika. You just lost Rosie."

"I know," Anika glances down at the two precious treasures, "but why should anyone else have to suffer such a loss, if I can prevent it." Delaney looks at the adults when the boys start crying again.

Daisy stares up at Allen with a flicker of hope, but he shakes his head. "This isn't our decision to make. We need to ask Glenn and Sue first."

"I'm sorry, to be selfish, Mrs. Coltrane, but the boys haven't much time left. I'll go get Glenn." Daisy runs from the room as fast her elderly feet can carry her. Allen moves forward and picks up one of the babies trying to soothe him.

Delaney reaches out and puts a finger in each tiny fist of the second baby, instantly calming him. He hiccups and tries to pull her hand into his mouth. "He's strong for such a tiny baby," she giggles.

Anika smiles and pats her daughter. "I learned with you just how strong a newborn can be. God fortified them for the journey of birth," she explains.

"But they need nourishment to help them grow stronger," a deep voice responds from behind her. Glenn Ward steps into the room and Anika loses all train of thought. He is massive, standing well over six feet two, muscular and blonde with a few days' growth of beard and red eyes from lack of sleep. Anika notices every detail, especially the red rimmed sky-blue eyes and worried expression on his face.

"I'm Glenn Ward. My mother tells me you can help us?"

"I'd like to try," Anika replies.

Glenn turns away from her to face Josiah. "Can you vouch for her health, Dr. Parker? Not to seem rude, but I have questions that need to be answered."

"No question about it, Mrs. Coltrane is very healthy. Her child's death was through no fault of hers." Dr. Parker insists. "Anika are you sure?" He asks worrying over her state of mind. The baby screams out and his sobs cause her to begin shaking again.

"It's just milk," Delaney snaps, "they need my Mama. Why is that so hard to see?"

"Delaney!" Anika says mortified, but Glenn laughs.

"I agree. I don't want to get Sue's hopes up. I'll tell her when she wakes. Let's give it a try."

Anika doesn't know whether to be relieved or not. "I'll stay and help with the boys." Daisy offers.

Dr. Parker nods, "Sue should sleep for a while, Glenn. The morphine will help," he explains.

Allen takes everyone downstairs to lunch, promising to feed Anika once the boys are settled.

"Delaney, you go with Mrs. Parker and eat. I'll be fine." She stands close to her mother, chewing on her lip with a distressed look. Anika settles into the rocking chair, while Daisy stands off to the side.

"Yes, Mama." Clara leads her out of the room talking to her about cherry juice.

Glenn stares at this young woman with the bruised body and feels guilty, but the thought of losing his boys forces him to push down his feelings and trust in the Lord. Picking up his son he hands him to Anika, "This is Quinton, he was the second born." Anika smiles softly as she finally gets to hold him. He fusses weakly while she settles him against her.

"His brother's name is Allen, after his grandfather," Daisy says rocking and patting him softly.

Anika looks down at the tiny baby with dark hair and flashes for a second to her Rosie. She closes her eyes and pushes back the pain as Quinton turns his head towards her and begins fussing in earnest. He can smell the rich milk waiting for him and Anika smiles up at Glenn with unshed tears in her eyes. "We'll send for you when they are full."

Glenn is shocked by the wave of pain he feels coming from her and he nods without speaking and walks out quickly.

Walking into the kitchen, he takes Dr. Parker aside and asks, "Tell me her story." Josiah pales and hesitates. Doctor patient confidentiality presses on him, but he sees a chance here for Anika and Delaney.

"Tell him, Josiah," Clara urges softly while Delaney plays with the dogs outside.

Anika struggles with the delicate task of unstrapping her gown and chemise, cradling Quinton in her arms. "I-I wasn't prepared to nurse," she explains, her voice uncertain.

"Let me get you a blanket and hold him while you get comfortable," Daisy offers, taking Quinton from Anika's arms and patiently waiting for her to settle.

"Thank you, I'm ready." Anika reaches for Quinton, but Daisy gasps, her eyes widening at the purple and black bruising marring Anika's ribcage. "It's okay,"

Anika blushes slightly in embarrassment, but all shame vanishes as accepts the baby and lifts him to her breast. Quinton latches on eagerly, and Daisy's heart swells with gratitude.

"That's right, little one, take what you need," Anika whispers as Daisy drapes a blanket over her shoulder and the baby, ensuring his tiny body stays warm. They share a laugh when he protests ten minutes later as she pulls him off to burp. Anika feeds him again for another ten minutes before burping once more. Aware that it's best not to let him consume too much during the first feeding, she slows him down, eliciting his protest, which startles his brother Allen.

Daisy takes Allen, swapping babies with Anika and walking with Quinton, praying he keeps the rich milk down. "Allen is bigger, but he seems to be struggling more than his brother," Daisy observes. Anika lifts Allen to her other breast, nodding in agreement.

"I'll make sure he takes his time, so he doesn't get an upset tummy. Delaney used to drink so fast her stomach would rebel." Quinton roots around for a moment before screaming and pushing away from her. His cold, sweaty skin alarms Anika, and she looks up at Daisy in concern.

"Daisy, this is going to sound strange, but could you help me undress him?" Daisy nods, swiftly stripping him to his cotton diaper and handing him back to Anika. She lays him against her body, skin to skin, and wraps the blanket over them. Making a shushing sound, Anika comforts him, and he stops fussing before rooting around and latching on, much like his brother. Anika sighs in relief; nursing is a welcome reprieve. She pauses every five minutes to pat and burp Allen.

"That's amazing. How did you know to do that?" Daisy asks, watching Quinton sleep contentedly for the first time since birth.

"My mother was a midwife in Virginia. I used to assist her with deliveries and follow-up visits. She encouraged the mothers to use skin-to-skin contact with the newborns. It soothed them and kept them warm."

"Does it pain you to feed them?" Daisy inquires, observing Quinton sleeping peacefully.

"It's actually a relief. It was becoming painful." Lifting Allen to her shoulder, she laughs as he drapes over her and burps softly. Anika inhales his sweet scent and presses a soft kiss to his tender cheek. Daisy lays him beside his brother, while Anika moves to the water basin to clean up and button her dress.

"I'll get the family." Daisy hurries from the room, struggling not to sob. She has never witnessed such a selfless act, and it touched her soul. With a quick swipe to her eyes, she finds them on the front porch watching Delaney and the dogs play.

Glenn leaps to his feet, taking his mother by the shoulders. Tears stream down her face, and she struggles to contain herself. "They rejected her?" he asks, his heart sore.

"No, forgive me, it's just... go see for yourself, son." Glenn drops his hands and hurries down the hall.

"Allen, it's a miracle. The boys took straight to her and are sleeping like... well... like babies." Her husband laughs and pulls her to his chest, pressing a kiss to her forehead.

"Listen, no screaming babies!" Allen teases, holding his wife tightly. "God is good."

Delaney watches quietly, glad that her Mama could

help, before one of the dogs distracts her with a game of chase.

Glenn knocks softly and pushes the door open with a trembling hand. Anika is rocking in the chair with her head back, resting. The creaking of the wooden rocker is the only sound in the room. The silence rocks him to his core as he walks over to the bassinet and stares in shock at his sons. They are side by side and sound asleep.

"It's called milk drunk, Mr. Ward. They did fine. So far, they have kept it down. I will feed them once more before we leave." Anika offers standing up gingerly, intending to go find her daughter.

"How will we ever thank you? You don't know..." his voice breaks, and Glenn turns away to walk to the window to compose himself.

"I do know." Anika turns away willing herself to move away from them. She knows Dr. Parker told him about her circumstances. "It makes my daughter's passing seem to have... meaning." Her voice is hoarse and raw with pain. "I know that God is in control and has a purpose for everything, but I couldn't see it clearly, until now. Rosie gave us all a gift today and for now, it will have to be enough."

Glenn doesn't try to stop his tears from falling as his sons sleep with full bellies for the first time since birth. "Their mother is dying, slowly, ebbing away from us." He turns back to look at her. "I believe she waits, to make sure they are going to be okay. I know it's a lot to ask, Mrs. Coltrane, but would you consider staying for a few days." Glenn wipes his eyes and hurries to stand in front of her and blurts out, "I would be willing to pay you whatever the going rate is, plus, room, board, and all your meals included."

Anika steps back in stunned silence. "You want to hire me?" The bruises stand out shockingly against her pale skin.

"Dr. Parker explained that you've just lost your husband and daughter and I know it must seem selfish of me to drop this on you, but I'm desperate. We have tried everything..." he rubs the back of his neck seeming to be at a loss for words for the first time since they've met.

Sitting slowly in the chair again, Anika is silent. "I don't know what to say," she murmurs looking at the cradle. The boarding house is paid in full, until the weekend and she has no idea what will happen after that. She had thought about being hired on as a maid or laundress, until she could find something else, but this... this would be perfect.

"I have to think of my daughter. It's a generous offer, but I would need Delaney's approval and I would like to talk to Dr. Parker." Anika doesn't wait, she leaves quickly before she makes a rash decision.

Walking out front she joins the family on the front porch and gives Delaney a quick hug. "Mama, the dogs love me, and they have cats too!" She stammers excitedly.

"Cats? We have more than cats, Delaney. We have goats, pigs, cow, sheep and even chickens," Allen says with a laugh. Delaney's eyes grow wide with excitement.

"Horses, Mr. Allen? Do you have horses too?" She gasps.

"Horses? Of course, we have horses. What kind of farmer doesn't have horses. In fact, we have a new foal named Starlight. If your Mother says yes, I can take you to meet her." Delaney whirls around and Anika smiles with gratitude.

"That would be wonderful. Obey, Mr. Ward,

Delaney." She watches her daughter in amazement as she hesitates before looking up at him. Allen reaches out and offers his hand causing Delaney to take a step back. She avoids his eyes, not quite ready to trust so easily.

"Follow me little lady, Starlight is waiting." Delaney giggles as she follows Allen and Anika sighs. This family would be good for her daughter to be around. Delaney would get to see how a man is supposed to treat his wife and daughter. Decision made she turns to Dr. Parker.

"I'll have your lunch brought out to you. Please sit down." Daisy leaves with Clara offering to help.

"Dr. Parker, exactly what did you tell Mr. Ward?" Anika asks.

"It seemed to me that God brought your two families together with a purpose in mind. I wouldn't put you and Delaney at risk. I explained that you lost your husband and newborn. Not why or how. I hope you don't mind, but this family is desperate. I've known them for years, Anika, you can trust them."

Anika is silent for a moment, "I trust your opinion. Will you help me negotiate terms? I want to make sure we are taken care of. I never want to be destitute again. I would hate to take advantage of their generosity or situation and I'm not sure what the going rate is for a wet nurse."

"Of course." Josiah is thrilled that she is considering it. "You, of course, would be taking on two babies. I believe you should be able to nurse them for as long as you are healthy and taking care of yourself. Delaney will thrive here, and these babies need you. Not to pressure you more than you already are, Anika, but you are the only chance they have at surviving."

Anika drops her head into her hands, trying to

block out the images of two innocent lives lost. "I never expected this day to end this way," she murmurs softly.

"I know, Anika. This could be exactly what you and Delaney need. Let me draw up the contract for you. I think they would agree to a trial period of a month and at the end of that time you can decide if the terms are agreeable."

"Thank you, Josiah. You and Clara have been so kind to us. I don't know how I will repay you." He takes her hand and squeezes gently.

"By using this time to heal. God's plan is not always clear or the path easy to walk, but I believe you will find peace."

"Thank you, I will try."

Daisy returns with a tray of food and fresh juice. Anika is starved and eats her fill while Daisy and Clara go inside to check on the boys. Josiah discusses details with Anika while she eats then walks inside to present the offer.

Anika waits for Delaney to return and smiles when she hears her excited chatter. "I love Starlight Mr. Allen, she is perfect. Do you really think I could ride her someday?"

"Of course, sugar. Now I'm going to leave you with your Mama and go see if I can find a cookie or two." Delaney watches him leave before turning to her Mother.

"I like Mr. Allen. He's nice, and the pony is perfect! Are you okay, Mama?" Delaney asks.

"I am fine, but I have a big question for you Delaney." Anika explains that they would like to hire her to care for the twins and Delaney glances out at the farm.

"We would stay here. With them?" Fear has her moving closer to her mother.

"Yes. They are good people, Delaney. The babies need us, and I could save enough to rent our own house soon. You will have your own room and proper lessons."

"Could I learn to ride a horse?" She asks with a little more excitement.

"I'm sure we could ask. Maybe, you could learn to care for some of the animals. What do you think?"

"I think... it would be okay with me, Mama."

Anika hugs her close and whispers to her. "Everything is going to be better now, Delaney. I promise."

***

"Look at them, sleeping like little angels," Daisy says, leaning into her husband. No one speaks of the relief of not listening to their screams grow weaker and weaker over the past few weeks.

"This is the first spark of hope in a long time," Allen says, looking at his son. "Will she stay?"

"I don't know, Dad. I hope so, and I haven't asked Sue yet. I'm not sure how she will feel about it," Glenn murmurs, thinking of his wife. Her pain was unbearable this morning, and her heart is stuttering. Breathing is becoming difficult for her, and she has refused food for the last two days. His biggest fear is that he will be burying them all together.

Dr. Parker knocks and enters to check the boys. He listens to their hearts and bellies, struggling to contain his excitement. "If they didn't reject her milk within the first few minutes, they are holding it." Turning to look at the family, he explains, "Glenn, Sue will be asleep for four to six hours. I will leave drops for you to keep her comfortable. Increase it as needed. I'm afraid I've done all I can for your wife. I don't expect her to make it through the night. I'm sorry to be so blunt."

"I understand," Glenn replies quietly.

"Hope waits for your sons, Glenn! Anika and Delaney are like family to Clara and me. She has agreed to a temporary stay for four weeks. If that is agreeable to you, I will act in Mrs. Coltrane's stead to negotiate terms with you for hiring her as your wet nurse."

All of them beam with relief and joy. "Oh, this is wonderful!" Daisy sits heavily in the rocker.

Glenn shakes his hand, "Thank you."

"Whatever it takes to make her stay, son, you know your mother and I will help in every way we can." Glenn can't speak. The emotion is too overwhelming. On the one hand, he is losing his wife and childhood friend, but he feels like he's been handed a miracle for his sons.

"You will all stay for dinner," Daisy says, and she hurries to go speak to the housekeeper.

"Before I agree to any terms, I will speak to Sue. Until she is able to meet Mrs. Coltrane, this is a temporary accord."

"Of course, let the boys sleep. When they wake, Anika will feed them again, and perhaps seeing your sons full and content will ease Sue's pain," Dr. Parker suggests.

Chapter 4

Anika hears the babies fussing and hurries into their room to find that Daisy and Clara have already changed them.

Glenn steps inside and clears his throat over the fussing boys. "Mrs. Coltrane, my wife would like to meet you, and she has asked if you would feed the boys in our room."

Delaney grips her hand as she stares at the large man with trepidation. "Of course, that would be fine," Anika replies.

"Me too, Mama." Delaney whispers.

"I will bring Allen. He seems to be demanding a little louder than his brother," Daisy laughs as she lifts the squalling baby. "Delaney, could you carry his blanket for me?"

Delaney nods, "Yes ma'am," and watches Glenn pick up Quinton before gently tucking him into his chest. "Come on then, can't let your brother win. I know a shortcut," he teases and winks at Delaney.

Anika follows swiftly behind Glenn with Delaney, and they are surprised to learn the house has two sets of stairs leading to the second floor. "In case of fire, we didn't want to be trapped with no second exit. It is also convenient for when guests are staying in the house."

Glenn leads the way and smiles when he hears his Mother behind them.

"Curse my short legs," Daisy sniffs as she falls in behind them. Delaney giggles, and Anika smiles down at her. They stop outside a door, and Glenn takes a deep breath before opening the door.

Sue Ward sits propped up in a dimly lit bedroom with her black hair around her shoulders. Her chocolate eyes stand out against the blue pallor of her skin. Glenn walks over to the window holding the baby and opens the curtain, allowing the sunset to cast a golden light on everything. Sue's rapid breathing indicates the struggle she is having just to breathe. Despite her condition, she smiles when she sees the family.

Dr. Parker steps away from Sue and touches Glenn's shoulder as he passes.

"Clara and I will be on our way home. I will come tomorrow to drop off Anika's things and check in on Sue." Clara hugs Anika before Josiah leaves, and Anika isn't sure how she feels about being left with virtual strangers.

"Sue, I'm not sure this is a good idea," Glenn starts to say, but she is intent on Anika.

"Glenn, I'd love some tea. I ..." she gasps, "have plenty of company until you return." Glenn pats Allen and turns away from his wife with a frown. He offers the baby to Anika, and he immediately starts rooting against her dress and fussing loudly. Quinton picks up on his brother's fussing, and both boys are soon screaming together. Glenn leaves to get her tea and stops outside the door to listen.

Anika smiles and sits in the rocking chair beside the bed. Daisy offers her a blanket, and Sue holds her breath as Anika removes the top of her dress revealing a worn camisole covering the bruises. Daisy props a pillow under her arm and hands the baby to her. Allen settles, and within seconds he latches on. The moment Allen stops screaming, Quinton calms down as if he knows he will be next.

Silence fills the room, and everyone sits in the peace that feeding them brings.

"I'm Anika Coltrane, and this is my daughter, Delaney." Anika smiles at Sue and runs a loving hand over Allen's dark hair.

"It's lovely... to... meet... you," Sue pants. Tears fill her eyes as she watches this stranger give life to her sons.

Delaney crowds close to her mother and smiles at the baby, "Poor lambs are hungry again, right Mama?" The awkwardness fades away as the women laugh.

"Newborns eat every few hours, well, at least you did," she says touching Delaney on the nose. She switches sides and struggles to keep some of her body covered while feeding the baby. Daisy offers to help.

"Your dress is nice, but it is not good for nursing," Daisy says. A blanket is placed over her shoulder to give her privacy, and Allen is placed against her skin. He immediately starts rooting and grunting before latching on.

"We shall have to remedy that soon," Daisy says with a nod of determination. Delaney goes still and stares at her mother as Allen latches on to feed.

"Allen, right?" Anika asks Sue.

"Yes, they look almost... identical, but he is bigger and has a dimple on his chin."

Delaney leans over her mother's shoulder to watch. Allen is drinking greedily and grunting. Delaney giggles. "He sounds like a little piggy. Does it hurt, Mama?" She asks softly.

Anika is quick to reassure her. "With the first child, it did because I didn't know what I was doing. I learned quickly. You were a great teacher, and now it actually feels good. If I don't feed every few hours, it becomes painful," Anika explains.

"Oh, that's not good." Delaney says staring at the infant in fascination. "Did Rosie look like this, Mama?" Anika looks up swiftly and nods no.

Glenn is just about to go downstairs when Delaney asks the question. He leans in closer to the door in the hallway to hear the answer.

"She was much smaller than this love. That's why she couldn't stay, but you understand she's in Heaven now. There is no pain in Heaven, only love."

"But Daddy is there, and he liked to give you pain, Mama. Will he hurt Rosie?" Anika struggles not to cry, but she knows this is important. She ignores the women in the room and answers the best way she can.

"No, because Daddy's heart has been healed, Delaney. All his pain and anger are gone now. The Bible says that God doesn't allow us to be hurt in heaven." Delaney isn't convinced, but she accepts the answer for now.

Glenn wipes away a tear as he struggles with the how's and why's of the situation they all find themselves in. Anger is boiling just beneath the fear, hurt, and pain. Unable to stand it, he storms off to make tea.

"Delaney, would you like to help me bake some cookies?" Daisy asks.

"Can I, Mama?" Delaney asks.

"Yes, Angel. Thank you, Daisy." Anika watches her daughter run over to Sue and touch her hand.

"Goodbye, Mrs. Sue," she says. Sue smiles and grips her hand.

"Thank you... for sharing your Mama, Delaney."

Delaney shrugs and says, "My Mama is the best."

Daisy places Allen beside his mother and hands Quinton to Anika before she guides her from the room. Sue carefully touches his little hand smiling when he grips her finger tightly.

Anika clears her throat as she avoids Sue's eyes. "My husband was damaged after the war. Whiskey, lager, moonshine, any kind of alcohol became his refuge, instead of me. I tried to be what he needed, but it only angered him more. He left us with next to nothing, and I would like to get Delaney away from the bad memories and give us time to heal."

Sue smiles at this young woman who has seen so much loss and suffering but still manages to put her daughter's needs before her own. Just as she did for their sons, her heart whispers.

Glenn returns with tea and is about to knock only to stop at Sue's words.

"I prayed for you, Anika. I prayed, and I held on..." she draws in a deep breath, "because I know that God doesn't allow pain without a reason." Tears flow freely now, and she is gasping for breath as she watches another woman feed her son.

"Don't try to speak, Sue, I will go get Glenn," Anika says but Sue shakes her head no and wipes at her eyes as she stands up and moves towards her.

"Let me... tell you." Panting, she pushes herself forward, desperate to be heard. "I didn't know..."

"You didn't know what, Sue?" Anika asks.

"I didn't know that he would take your daughter to

save my sons... forgive me," she pleads.

The teacups shutter on the tray as the gravity of her words strikes Glenn in his heart. He leans back against the hallway wall and bows his head in horror.

Anika lays Quinton on the bed, buttons her dress, and takes Sue's hand. "No. Rosie died because my husband savagely beat me. I was too weak to save her, but you fought and saved them. Your boys are a gift. Look at them, Sue."

They are laying stretched out beside each other, and their mouths move as if still sucking. Sue smiles through her tears. "God gifted you with two beautiful sons, and they will grow in grace. You can rest knowing they are strong, healthy, and loved." Sue leans back and clasps her hand.

"I want to... hold them. Will you help... me?" Her breathing is growing shallower, and Anika hurries to help her.

"Of course," she murmurs.

Glenn steps into the room and sucks in a breath. Sue is vibrating with excitement as she looks at her babies.

Anika ignores Glenn's presence and moves quickly to help her. She props a pillow under each arm and tucks both boys against their mother. One in each arm.

"This is the first time... I could hold them without the screaming." Sue stares in awe at each baby. "They are so beautiful. I did good, didn't I?"

"You did amazing," Anika replies with a tremulous smile.

"Thank you for coming." Sue looks up and smiles.

"I'll leave you with your husband now." Anika moves to the door and stops when Sue calls out to her.

"You are wrong Anika, calling yourself weak." Her voice grows stronger, and she leans forward, "When I go to Heaven, I will find her, your Rosie, and I will tell her about her mother with the big heart. I will love her with all that I am."

Anika's tears can't be held back as she rushes past Glenn and into the hallway. Sobs rip from the depths of her soul, and she can only stumble into a guest room to cry out to her God.

"Help me understand," she whispers in the dark.

Chapter 5

"Glenn," Sue struggles to catch her breath, "I need to tell you..." she gasps in pain and closes her eyes.

"Let me take the boys," but she immediately squeezes them closer to her body with her frail arms.

"NO!" Sue starts coughing, and Glenn grabs the drops off the nightstand and pours a spoonful as instructed. When her spell subsides, he offers her the medicine and tries to stop the trembling of his hands.

"Thank you," she whispers. Glenn grabs a cloth and dips it in the bowl next to the bed. He wipes her mouth, smiling when she closes her eyes at his gentle touch.

"I wish..." she looks at him, "I wish I could stay with you. Glenn, please don't be mad at me."

Glenn stretches out beside her on the bed with an arm around her shoulder and stares down at their sons resting in her loving embrace. "How could I ever be mad at you, Sue. You gave me two miracles." Sue turns her face and rests her head on his shoulder.

"I wanted you, Glenn. When we were children, I would watch you..." her voice fades as the memories flash. "So tired," she murmurs, and her eyes close for a second. Her breathing is labored, and her skin is ice-cold.

"Rest, then. Don't try to talk," he pleads.

"No time," she mumbles. "I knew it was wrong, to love you. I was never for this world. I just wanted to know love before..." Glenn lifts her chin and kisses her silent.

"You are loved."

She sighs and smiles against his mouth. "Liar." Her brown eyes open wide, and she is frantic for a moment. "Promise me that you will not let anger grow in your heart."

Tears fill his eyes as he stares at her. "I promise, Sue." She relaxes at his words.

"Talk to me, Glenn."

"Close your eyes, my love." Sue presses a kiss to each dark head, smiling at the contented sounds.

"The sun is shining, Sue, and if you listen, you can hear them teasing each other. Grass and dirt fly up into the air as they race across the field on two horses. Identical brown-haired boys, laughing and racing to see who can get back to the barn first. The dogs chase behind them, barking and trying their best to keep up. They are strong, healthy, and rambunctious... do you see them, Sue?"

Sue smiles and nods. Her breathing grows slower as her heartbeat stutters and stops for the last time. One moment she is struggling to stay, and the next all her pain is gone. Looking down on the man she loves and her children, she feels the light of God surround her as he calls her home. It is warm, loving and waiting. When she turns to go, all worry, fear, and guilt are wiped away as she runs freely into the arms of Heaven.

Glenn feels the moment her heart stops but can't bring himself to let go of her just yet. He prays that God will guide his wife home and help him be the man he needs to be.

"Go in peace, my Angel."

Chapter 6

Anika keeps the boys in the nursery upstairs during the wake and funeral. The doctor believes they are still too weak to be exposed to that many people, and she is relieved. Sue was loved by the Ward family and a large church family, but she is still healing herself.

On the third night after Sue's funeral, Quinton's cries wake her. Though her bruises have healed some, her ribs and back still cause her trouble. She moves as quickly as her body will allow her to. Delaney sleeps soundly in the double bed they share as she grabs her wrapper. Quietly, she pulls the door cracked to their room so Delaney can sleep.

"Hey little man," Anika calls softly. His cries slow when he hears her voice, and she smiles gently as she reaches in and places a hand on his belly. Chilled, she pulls her wrapper over her chemise and whispers, "No need to work yourself up, I'm here." Quinton kicks his feet and begins rooting around on his fist. As she lifts him to her shoulder, he turns his little face towards her cheek, and she giggles when he tries to suck on her face.

"Sweet boy," she coos, and just as she turns towards the rocker, a shape looms in front of her, causing her to clutch the baby protectively to her chest. Anika doesn't scream but instead curves over the child, turning partly away, with her eyes squeezed tight and waits for the first blow.

"Easy now. I didn't mean to scare you, Mrs. Coltrane. I heard his cries and came to help." Glenn lights the oil lamp on the side table and stares at her as she attempts to control her shaking.

Mortified, Anika straightens up and faces him in the soft glow. "I'm so sorry... I didn't know you were in here." Quinton begins to fuss, causing Anika to pat him and walk the floor on trembling legs. Allen hears his brothers cries and wakes at the same moment.

"No apologies needed." Glenn looks away, not sure if she realizes the picture she presents in that moment. Dressed in a tattered white dressing gown and wrapper which has clearly seen better days, bruised and embarrassed, yet willing to protect his sons. Anika is a puzzle to him. He picks up Allen and ignores the way her golden-red hair ripples around her shoulders. "I'll just take Allen and change him, knock on my door when you have fed Quinton and we will switch. Does that sound alright?"

"Yes, thank you." Glenn hurries from the room, and a sigh of relief escapes her. Thirty minutes later, she returns Quinton to his cradle after changing him. Full and content, he sleeps soundly.

"Better get on with it then," she whispers to herself as she crosses the hall as quietly as she can. Thankfully, the other family members are on the other side of the house. A quick rap on the door, and he whispers for her to enter.

Opening the door, she sees Glenn in a wingback chair holding a content baby. He is awake and staring up at his Daddy.

"I can take him now, so you can sleep." She crosses to him and stops when she realizes that she is alone with him in his bedroom in the middle of the night.

"I don't sleep much these days." He yawns and looks at her standing in the middle of his room with her large wide eyes. "We will be spending a great deal of time together, Mrs. Coltrane. To damn with propriety, you can't possibly care for two infants in the middle of the night alone," he holds up a hand when she begins to protest.

"I only wish to help, and I've hardly spent any time with them since they were born. Most of my time was spent caring for my sick wife and working the orchard." Glancing down at his son, he touches his cheek gently, "I almost lost them, so forgive me if I seem too forward." He stands up and walks towards her, and she forces herself to not back away. Glenn watches the fear flicker across her face for an instant before she tamps it down.

"You and Delaney will never have to fear for your safety under my roof. That is a promise." Her eyes study his face, a scruffy beard, with red stress-streaked eyes, and behind the exhaustion, an anger for her. Anika is speechless as she reaches for Allen. Holding him close to her body, she turns to walk to the door and pauses to turn back and stare at Glen.

"Thank you, I... I don't know what to say to that. My husband promised to love, honor, and protect me, none of which he did. So, you'll forgive me if I seem jaded." Anika stares at him with a challenge in her eyes and turns to leave.

"Sue was right, you know." Glenn says and runs a hand through his hair, stopping her in her tracks.

"Right about what, Mr. Ward," Anika asks as she

pivots to look at him.

"About you not being weak. I don't think I've ever met a woman with the strength I see in you. Delaney is lucky to have you, and so are my boys."

Touched beyond words, Anika smiles. "Thank you for saying so, though I don't feel very strong these days. I'm hoping to change that."

"Perhaps we could both use a friend. Call me, Glenn."

Anika doesn't hesitate to reply. "I could use a friend and since we've blown all sense of respectability out the window, you may call me, Anika."

Glenn smiles for the first time in months and watches her leave. He returns to his chair and picks up his Bible, intending to read, but finds he can't quite bring himself to open the book. It is almost impossible to understand how that gentle woman could have been put through so much. The past five years of his life have been hellish, and he will not lie to himself and say he isn't questioning his faith. His wife is buried only three days now, and he is having feelings for a woman he barely knows. Is this another test? Anger boils, and he stamps it back down. Sleep will not come easy this night. Later, as he rides out of the barn he is unaware that the woman rocking and feeding his son, is wondering the same thing.

Chapter 7

They came when the call went out that Sue had passed away. For the next three weeks, neighbors brought food, offered services, and did whatever they could to ease her passing. Anika saw some familiar faces from church and some new. She was treated with trepidation by the younger female members of the church and invited to attend when the children were strong enough by the older families.

Anika glances at the mirror in the house; all of them are covered with black mourning cloths, every surface of the home seemed to be in mourning. It's a shocking difference when compared to Saul's funeral. Anika glances at Delaney playing with a doll and smiles as she nurses Quinton. They share a large bedroom connected to the nursery, which makes caring for the twins easier. Her favorite feature is the window seat, with its beautiful view of the land facing the front of the house. Often, she sits and quilts at night when Delaney is sleeping.

The Ward family has been spoiling Delaney, and she is blossoming now that the fear is diminished. Children rebound quickly, and her nightmares are not as frequent.

Beneath the sadness of losing Sue is an undercurrent of joy at having two grandsons who are thriving. Daisy offered to help with the boys in the middle of the night, but Anika insisted that she get caught up on sleep. The boys are putting on weight quickly now that regular meals are available. Daisy spoils Anika, feeding her often and insisting she rest and recuperate. Anika smiles down at Quinton and grins when she realizes healing is a family affair in this house.

Glenn's nightly visits have become routine. Anika doesn't complain; he merely takes one of the boys and lets her have her privacy, until they switch. They whisper in the dark of simple subjects, the farm, the orchards, and the children. The bags under his eyes grow deeper, his clean-shaven face is covered in a week's worth of growth, and he is angry all the time. Often his knuckles are bandaged, and he has bruises on his face that he doesn't bother explaining. Everyone notices, but no one speaks of it, hoping that he will figure out a way to deal with it soon.

Dr. Parker is thrilled at how well the boys are doing and encourages Anika to continue sleeping, eating, and feeding the babies. Daisy has made sure to keep her fed, and Allen has been teaching Delaney how to care for some of the farm animals.

Anika finishes with Quinton and lays him in the wooden cradle with his brother before stepping to the window to enjoy the evening sunset. The bruises on her face are gone while her body is still recovering from the abuse. Not to mention childbirth and nursing twins. Feeding two babies is a challenge, but she is determined to get them on a schedule instead of nursing them every hour.

Glenn is walking back from the barn and glances up at her window as if sensing her presence. He frowns and touches the tip of his hat, and the black cloth round his arm reminds her of his loss. Work has become his saving grace. Exhaustion beats at him, but he finds sleep elusive, so he rides, works, and works more. Delaney is ever watchful of him, as if she senses the rage boiling in his soul. As Anika stares into his eyes, her heart weeps for him, this man who has been through so much. She presses a hand to her stomach and decides the strange feeling in her stomach must be hunger. They break eye contact at the sound of horses.

A carriage comes rumbling down the dirt lane. Glenn smiles for the first time in a week when the door opens. A young woman leaps down, ignoring respectable protocol and runs flinging herself into his open arms, knocking her hat from her head revealing red hair.

Pushing back from his bear hug she snaps, "Let me breathe, you moose," and they laugh as she grabs his face and looks into his eyes. "I'm so sorry, Glenn, I came as soon as I could."

"Thank you. God, it's good to see you. Let's go inside."

Anika frowns as they walk away arm in arm and reminds herself that it's none of her business. "I just work here."

"Mama, who are you talking to?" Delaney asks looking up from her book.

"No one, sweets."

"Delaney, are you happy here?" She asks.

"Yes, Mama. I'm sad that Mrs. Sue had to go, but I'm happy we get to stay. You won't leave me, will you Mama?" She asks twirling her long dark curls.

"Come here, Delaney." Delaney moves into her mother's loving embrace, and they sit on the window seat. This has become a daily question in the last week. "Mrs. Sue was sick for a long time, and I'm not sick."

"I know, Mama, but I don't want to lose you." Delaney sniffs, Anika hugs her close and closes her eyes, sending a quiet plea to find the right words to comfort her daughter.

"Delaney, I can't promise I won't die, because that is one thing that we all have to walk through someday. What I can promise you is that you will never be alone." Anika pushes Delaney back and looks into her eyes. "The book of Joshua says, 'Be strong and courageous, do not be afraid, do not be discouraged, for the Lord your God will be with you wherever you go,' and that means you are never alone."

Delaney smiles and hugs her tight. "I like that. Can I go see Mrs. Daisy now? I am through with my lesson."

Anika nods with relief and sighs as Delaney skips from the room. The fear Delaney carries is a mirror image of the fear weighing her down. Allen stirs and begins to fuss. Anika picks him up and lifts him to her shoulder, patting him gently.

"You can't be hungry already, piggy." He burps loudly, causing her to giggle.

"That's a beautiful sound to a Father's ear." Anika turns slowly to greet Glenn and his visitor.

Anika smiles softly, "You're just in time to visit with them."

"Anika Coltrane, I'd like to introduce you to Savannah Ward, my sister." Savannah steps forward, eager to see the babies and meet the woman who saved them.

Sister, of course. The resemblance is in the coloring and blue eyes. Anika hides her surprise and relief. Saul wasn't faithful during their marriage, and her anger at him grows when she realizes how he has colored every aspect of her life. She is ashamed when she realizes she automatically assumed Glenn was the same way.

"It's a pleasure to meet you, Mrs. Coltrane." Savannah's eyes drop to baby Allen draped across her shoulder. Tears flood her eyes, and she covers her mouth with a hand.

"Please, call me Anika. Would you like to hold him?"

Savannah glances up at Ward and takes a step back, only to have her brother gently shove her. "Don't tell me you're afraid of a tiny baby?"

"It's just he's so small, Ward." Savannah stares at Anika with a blush of embarrassment. They are the same age, yet here she is caring for three children.

"Oh, he's growing by the day. Quinton is the smallest, but he's very strong," Anika encourages her. Glenn moves over to pick him up. He seems even smaller held against such a large man.

"They're so beautiful," Savannah wipes her eyes with a cloth.

"Alright, peanut, you promised no tears," Glenn wraps an arm around her shoulder and pulls his sister into his side.

"Look at him," Savannah reaches out a trembling hand and touches a tiny fist. "He's perfect," she murmurs.

"Yes," Anika whispers, wondering if Savannah is speaking about the baby or the man. He is so gentle, despite his size. Saul almost erased the memory of how a man should treat women.

Glenn's blue eyes stare at Anika as Allen turns his face into hers, rooting around as if still hungry, and buries a small fist in her strawberry blonde curls. Anika smiles and presses a kiss to his temple. He sighs against her and settles back down.

"I'll try, but you have to stay, Glenn," Savannah says, breaking him free of his reverie. He nods and guides Savannah to a chair. "I'll hold Allen first," she nods at him and grins. "He's a moose, like his daddy." Glenn laughs as Anika walks over and places him in her arms.

"Just remember to support the head with the crook of your arm or if you lift him to your shoulder, support the back of his head. He isn't strong enough to do that, yet." As she moves to step away, Allen's fist closes tightly in her curls.

"Oh!" Anika laughs softly as she untangles her hair. "He has developed a thing for my hair; he buries his fist in it every time I hold him."

Glenn steps forward and grins. "I can't say I blame him. It looks like spun gold when the light hits it."

Anika straightens in shock, blushes, and stammers. "I, I, I'll leave you to visit and go save Daisy from Delaney's help in the kitchen." She hurries from the room.

"Glenn!" Savannah stares in open-mouthed shock at her brother. "You can't speak to her like that."

"Like what? It was just an observation." He pats Quinton and sits near his sister in the window seat. "I meant no harm, Savannah."

"No harm! If someone else heard, you speak like that… well, you know perfectly well the conclusion they would jump to. You just keep those kinds of thoughts to yourself."

"People can get stuffed." He glowers at her. "Those

same people did nothing while her husband beat her. I don't give a da..."

"Glenn!" Savannah gawks at him. "You need her to stay, and if you scare her, she might leave."

"I'm sorry." Glenn stares out the door after Anika. "You have a good point."

Savannah nuzzles the baby and smiles. "Tell me everything you know about her." Savannah watches his face as he tells her the story. His voice grows hoarse as he shifts Quinton to a pillow on his lap.

"There are no words to explain her selfless act, Savannah." She listens to how they met, and the way he speaks of her has her heart sighing.

Glancing out of the bedroom window, she wonders what God has in store for these two broken souls. In that moment, her decision is made. "I've come home for good, Glenn. I want to be here to help and watch the boys grow. Do you mind?"

He grins with excitement. "Of course not, I've been praying for you to come home. I'd feel better having you here. It would allow Mom and Dad to move back to the main house."

"Good luck with that. I can't imagine them wanting to leave these two."

Glenn laughs and touches his sister's hand. "I've missed you, Savannah."

"I missed you too. How are you handling things?"

Glenn's smile fades, and he clears his throat. "I'm okay. We should go tell Dad and Mom the good news. Don't drop him." He stalks from the room holding Quinton, and she watches him go.

"Daddy's hurting, little man. War, death, and destruction have stained his soul. We have to pray hard that God will wash him clean." Savannah presses a kiss and follows him from the room.

Anika watches Daisy work with Delaney, mixing the cookie dough and laughs as they tease each other. Her heart clenches at the thought of her mother teaching her how to make the family recipes.

"Come help Mama," Delaney calls and lifts a flour-covered hand.

"Oh, no. Last time you got it all over my dress." Laughing, she looks at Daisy. "I do miss baking, though. I used to bake with my mother."

"Really? What did you make with your Mama?" Delaney calls as she presses the cookie down out of the way Daisy showed her.

"We would make so many things, Delaney. Mama would sell her pies, cakes, and cookies in town. Every year we would spend a few weeks baking, and the house would smell heavenly."

Daisy smiles wistfully. "I used to cook with Savannah too."

"True, but Savannah's weren't exactly edible," Glenn says from the doorway.

Savannah shoves past him and snaps, "Don't listen to him, Delaney, the cows loved my cookies."

Delaney isn't sure what to think of the light-hearted banter, but she can't stifle a giggle at them.

"I'd love to have some help in the kitchen, Anika. We are about to have a bounty of apples. Picking season starts soon, and we usually have a bake sale," Daisy suggests.

"Oh, maybe I should have come back home after

picking season." Savannah sniffs and explains, "Picking season is our busiest time of year."

Anika grins, "What do you bake, Daisy?"

"Anything and everything. The proceeds go to the church." Daisy pulls the first batch of cookies from the oven while Delaney dances around the grownups.

"I'd be glad to help. I have my mother's recipes, and I'd love to bake again."

"Don't forget my favorites..." Glenn starts to say, but Allen steps into the room and calls out loudly.

"Oh, no you don't, Son. My favorites first." Daisy smiles at her husband as he presses a loud kiss to her cheek. Delaney has moved to the back wall to watch quietly. Anika moves close to her and smiles when the little hand presses into hers.

"Story time, Delaney?" Anika murmurs softly. Delaney nods and pulls her gently from the room.

"Excuse us, please."

Glenn watches them go, and the teasing nature of the room changes. "How's Anika doing, Mom?"

Daisy pulls the second sheet of cookies from the oven and sighs. "Dr. Parker said she needs to rest, eat, and heal. The true problem is keeping her from cleaning and chores. I've told her we have help, but she is used to doing that herself to earn her keep. I offered to hire a nanny to help care for the boys, but she wouldn't hear of it. You, of all people, know how hard it is to let your body heal."

Glenn rubs his arm absently, thinking of the gunshot wound that brought him home from the war after serving two years. He was lucky that it only winged him. Many others weren't so lucky. For a moment, he is back on the battlefield, and he can smell the metallic scent of death. Daisy touches his shoulder gently and reaches for the baby. She takes him with a sigh of contentment.

"I remember, Mama. It reminds me daily, but Anika will have to learn that she doesn't have the final say in everything. I will have a talk with her. I'm sure she will agree to having help a few days a week to let her heal. We will make sure she doesn't overdo it. I will be busy during the next few weeks with picking. Dr. Parker will be here tomorrow evening to go over the contract. I believe we are all in agreement that Anika and Delaney should stay. In fact, I asked him to make one change, and I hope Anika agrees. I had him list her as the boys' nanny." He turns to his father to grab coffee and cookies. "Speaking of picking, how many pickers will we have this year?" Father and son drift to the front porch to talk business while Savannah stays to visit with her mother.

"Nanny?" Daisy thinks about this change and can barely contain her smile. "I like it. It will give her a better standing in the community and it gives all of us a sense of security."

"Do you think she'll agree to it?" Savannah nibbles on a cookie.

"I think she is a smart young woman. She has become attached to the boys already. It will make it easier on all of us."

"I imagine it is uncomfortable having a stranger living in your home and taking care of your sons." Savannah sits at a small table and shifts the baby to her shoulder.

"It isn't, actually. Every time I look at her, I see a miracle, and Delaney is a delight. Savannah, we were so close to losing them all," she explains huskily.

"Oh, Mama. I'm so sorry I wasn't here to help, but

I'm home now. I'm staying for good."

Daisy gasps and reaches out a hand to clasp her daughter's tightly. "Truly?"

"Truly." She smiles and presses a small kiss to the baby's head. "I've seen enough death and destruction. I want to see life now. To watch them grow and spend time with my family."

"That is the best news, Savannah. What about your photography?"

"I've spent the past four years taking pictures of Soldiers, wounded or dead. Families rebuilding after the war and I've seen things that have changed me." Her eyes seek her mothers. "I can only thank you and Dad for allowing me the gift of this time. It has made my walk with the Lord that much stronger. When Glenn is ready, I will show him some of the images."

Daisy sighs, "He's angry, Savannah. Angry at Sue and her mother, God rest her soul. Angry at God and even more so at himself. I'm not sure what it will take to help him get over that."

Savannah smiles, "I've learned, Mom, that God's plans are not possible to discern. The best way to fight a battle is on our knees in prayer."

"Now my youngest is quoting Bible verses. Thank you. I needed to hear that. We should put these two to bed, and get you settled. We have a busy day ahead of us tomorrow."

"Why busy?" Savannah asks as she follows her mother upstairs.

"Tomorrow, Mrs. Flannagan is coming to help dress Anika and Delaney. You're just in time to help with that." Daisy grins as Savannah laughs.

"Poor Anika, she won't know what hit her."

"I want her to enjoy the experience. I'm hoping once they are all strong enough she will join us at church. Her husband didn't leave her with much and its one small way I can repay her for... everything."

Savannah nods thinking of her own trunks. "I'd love to help. I may have some dresses that could be altered to fit her, until the new ones are ready. Delaney will need dresses too. This will be fun, and we will make sure they are taken care of." Daisy tucks the boys into their beds and smiles down at them.

"God has blessed us. We may have lost Sue, but He gifted us with Anika and Delaney. We will make them feel cherished."

"That's your specialty, Mama."

Chapter 8

Delaney dances around her mother in excitement. "Do I get a new dress too, Mama?"

"Yes, you do," Daisy says with a big smile.

"Daisy, this isn't necessary." Anika tries for the third time to change her mind. Daisy sets up her prized sewing machine in the small bedroom across from the Master. "We shouldn't be in Glenn's room." They are currently standing in the master bedroom and Daisy is busy placing a step stool on the wooden floor.

"It's the largest of the rooms and has the most windows," Savannah explains.

"Winter is coming and this wee lass has outgrown that frock, to be sure." Mrs. Flannagan's Irish accent is strong, and Delaney giggles.

"You talk funny. What's a frock?" Delaney announces while Mrs. Flannagan looks properly shocked.

"Do I now? Step up here for me, so I can take your measurements." Delaney jumps up on the stool and claps her hands in excitement.

Savannah covers a grin and looks over her coloring. Delaney has chocolate hair, hazel eyes, and a beautiful complexion. "Mrs. Flannagan, she will need four-day dresses with undergarments, two tea dresses, shoes, stockings, nightclothes, a coat, and one Christmas dress," she recites. "She's lovely. I would think a beautiful rose-colored silk," Savannah asks Anika.

"Like this?" Martha, her twenty-year-old assistant, holds up a bolt of the silk and places a darker tone, velvet across it.

"Oh, that's lovely," Anika replies.

"A Christmas dress! Mama did you hear that?" Delaney's eyes are wide with excitement, and Anika can't help but smile in response.

"Yes, love." She looks at Savannah, who nods and continues writing down the measurements Mrs. Flannagan calls out. Anika glances at her own tattered brown dress, knowing the image she represents and remembering what it was like to feel proud of one's clothes. There was a time when she lived at home that she had the most beautiful dresses.

"Don't fret so, Mrs. Coltrane. The undergarments and shoes will come from the general store in town. They're carrying them in stock this time of year. The dresses will be custom-made, though I took the liberty of bringing one or two that I thought might work for Delaney. We were lucky that Miss Martha volunteered to help today. She is amazing with a sewing machine." Anika turns to look at Martha and can't help but smile slightly. She is overdressed for a seamstress and can't stop looking out the windows. Glenn will find her lovely with her dark blonde ringlet curls pulled up on the sides with bangs. Anika doubts she is wearing a peach, low-cut, calling dress for her sake. It's beautiful with the lace-trimmed ruffles, tiny waist, and bustle. Jealousy curls inside her, and she is quick to stomp it down.

The past week has been eye-opening with the

number of women callers bringing food to the house. Glenn just buried his wife. Do they really think he is ready to start courting? Anika isn't sure if they were coming to check her out or flirt with Glenn, but they let her know that she was no threat. With the war, so many women were left widows, and if he is ready, then it's none of her business, she reminds herself again.

"It's my pleasure. I'll get started on those straight away," Martha gives a pinched smile and takes the two dresses, then moves across the hall to the small room to get started.

"Now, it's your turn, Mrs. Coltrane."

"Please, call me Anika." She chews on her bottom lip and stares at Daisy. "You've done so much already, I'm not sure."

Savannah loops an arm through hers and guides her to the stool. "It won't hurt a bit. If it makes you feel any better, I'm next."

"May the Saints save us, not you too?" Mrs. Flannagan teases loudly, causing Daisy to giggle.

"Savannah is particular," she explains.

Savannah gasps in feigned indignation. "Whatever do you mean?" Anika laughs at their behavior, knowing it is for her benefit.

"Do ya remember the denims?" Mrs. Flannagan demands.

"Remember, I still have them. A sheer work of art, Mrs. Flannagan. In fact, I may need to have you make me a few more." Savannah presses a quick kiss to her wrinkled cheek.

"Hm, we'll see." She swiftly begins to take Anika's measurements. "You and Savannah are almost the same size, though she is taller than you with a few more pounds on her, but I'm sure Daisy's cooking will fix that up."

"I will ignore that jab at my weight, Mrs. Flannagan," Savannah sniffs and claps her hands together. "I have two dresses that I'm hoping you could alter for Anika today. I know they aren't perfect for nursing, but one is a two-piece dress, and the other has a short jacket that fits over the top. I think it could be lovely on Anika."

Savannah brings over a lilac-colored day dress with cream lace trimming and a second visiting dress made of colonial blue silk.

"Yes, that could work. Anika will have to try them on."

"They are lovely, but I should wear the proper mourning colors," Anika exclaims.

"Of course, we thought of that." Mrs. Flannagan shakes her head to reassure her. "I brought separate skirts, one black, one navy, with matching fitted jackets for you to wear over top of white blouses. These blouses are made for nursing mothers. The new corsets are padded for comfort and protection." Mrs. Flannagan shows Anika how they work and reassures her that it is what all the new mothers are wearing.

"I had no idea. This will make nursing the boys much easier." Anika inspects them and smiles excitedly. "I don't see why I would need anything else."

Savannah is quick to stop her.

"You will, of course, be joining us for church when the boys are old enough. We will have the bake sale, Thanksgiving, and Fall Carnival all coming up, not to mention Christmas. This is our busy social season, and we want you to feel like part of the family."

"Anika, Glenn is insisting that the clothing for you and Delaney be part of your salary. You will be representing our family when we have guests or go out. It is quite common, according to Dr. Parker," Daisy explains. "I'm sure he will go over the details with you this evening."

"I see. If that is the case, then of course, I accept your generous offer," Anika smiles and pushes back the shame that threatens. "Thank you."

"Perfect. Let's get on with it. I have something in mind for you. It's a midnight blue silk, Savannah." Mrs. Flannagan gestures to Savannah, who digs through a trunk and pulls out a five-piece outfit.

Anika gasps and touches the soft silk.

"Mourning colors have changed. Ya no longer have ta wear only black or brown. This will complement your hair color and your eyes. Try it on; I will be able to pin it and make the alterations."

Daisy helps unbutton the back of her dress, and when Anika walks over to the master bed to strip it off, she is unaware of the look on the ladies' faces. Dropping her old corset and undershirt, her bruises stand out harshly against the paleness of her skin. She misses Daisy shaking her head at Savannah, who is quick to wipe a tear from her face.

Anika has lost all the baby weight. She looks almost frail standing in the mid-morning sun. Her spine has a mottled look with yellow and green bruises. The largest of the bruises wraps around under her ribs is still light purple, though it too is beginning to fade.

"I'm going to get us some refreshments," Savannah says hoarsely and rushes from the room. Anika pulls on a cotton top with a new corset, followed by the bustled petticoat before she turns around slowly and looks at the two older women. Understanding flickers in Anika's eyes.

In a soft voice, "I'd nearly forgotten, forgive me ladies. The bruising is much better now. They're merely yellow and green, not purple, and black. Dr. Parker said it is normal to heal slowly after childbirth and nursing two babies. I seem to be asking a lot of my body, but soon they will be fade altogether."

"You must have been in so much pain, Anika. How did you ever manage to hold the boys against you?" Daisy asks softly.

"Pillows help. They are tiny yet. I plan on remedying that soon," she teases.

Mrs. Flannagan looks at her with new eyes. "Ya have a mighty spirit for such a wee thing," she walks over to her and begins tugging the strings. "This corset straps on the sides which allow for growth. If ya lose weight, not that ya need too, or gain weight, you can adjust it for comfort. Keep it loose until you heal."

Savannah rushes into the kitchen and struggles to regain her composure. She pours juice into glasses and adds biscuits with trembling fingers onto a serving tray. When Glenn enters from the back door, she is quick to wipe at her cheeks. His eagle eyes miss nothing.

"What's wrong?" Glenn demands.

"I wasn't prepared, I mean, I- I know about her past, but I wasn't ready," Savannah stammers. "I don't know how she can put pressure against her ribs and she holds both boys!"

"What are you talking about?"

"The bruises, Glen! They rain over her back and around her ribs. How could he do that to her?" Tears stream down her face as he curses and stalks out of the room. "What are you... Glenn, don't you dare!" Savannah races to the opposite staircase and runs up holding her skirt high and leaps in front of him.

"Dang peanut, I forgot how fast you are." He grins and tries to step around her.

"What is wrong with you?" Savannah hisses and shoves at his chest. "You can't go in there!"

"It's my home, Savannah." He once again tries to sidestep her only to find her blocking him again.

"Yes, but she isn't your wife."

Glenn pales, and Savannah whispers, "I'm sorry, Glenn, but Dr. Parker will be here soon. He will check her over and make sure she's healing properly. I just wasn't aware of how bad it was. Now, please go back downstairs."

Glenn glowers at her and nods, before turning and stomping away. Savannah sighs in relief and follows slowly thinking about Glenn's reaction to her words. To say it was unexpected would be a serious understatement.

A smile lights up her face, and she whispers, "He has feelings for her!"

Chapter 9

Martha glares at Savannah's retreating back from the doorway in the hall. She returns to the small room they stuffed her in. As she sews, she begins to plan. "Feelings! I've waited months for that woman to die, and now some woman thinks she's going to take him from me." Martha hisses in frustration when the thread jams in the machine. "No, this won't do."

All the women at church talk about what a great catch Glenn Ward would make. His business is booming with the advancements of the refrigerated rail cars. He can ship fruit all over the country. It will afford her the lifestyle she has dreamed of for herself. If this Anika hadn't rushed in to save the day, she would be consoling Glenn over losing his family, the way she had been planning. Now things will have to change.

"Is it finished yet?" Delaney asks, entering the bedroom at a run, causing Martha to jump in surprise.

"Do you run everywhere, child?" Martha snaps.

"Yes. Mama says I'm lucky I have long legs. It makes me fast."

"Perhaps your Mama should teach you that a lady doesn't run."

"I run, and I'm a perfect little lady. Mrs. Daisy says so." Delaney spins and claps her hands with excitement.

"Well, isn't that something," Martha says sarcastically and returns to her sewing while Delaney plays in the room.

"Mama and I are going to help with the bake sale for the church. Do you cook, Miss Martha?"

"No, I have people who cook for me," she says, suddenly interested in the child's yammering. "You could wear this new dress for the sale. Let's try it on while you tell me all about this bake sale."

Delaney claps her hands and rushes over excited to try on her new dress.

A half hour later Daisy calls out, "Tea is served in the living room, Mrs. Flanagan. You and Martha should join us downstairs while Anika changes."

Anika waits for them to leave and tries on a black bustled skirt, white shirt, and matching short black jacket that Mrs. Flannagan was able to easily fit to her body. Glancing in the mirror, she frowns at the reflection staring back at her. Her pale skin stands out even more strikingly against such a dark color. Savannah was able to convince her to let her do her hair. She pulls up the sides and curls it, leaving her natural curls about her shoulder, and a black choker completes the final look. Clean, professional, and... boring.

"Perfect. Exactly as it should be. You're not here to win the affections of anyone," Anika says to herself in the mirror. "Just you remember that."

Dr. Parker and wife, Clara, are waiting in the sitting room for her, along with Daisy, Savannah, Mrs. Flannagan, and Martha. Delaney is spinning around in her new dress, showing off in excitement. "Oh, Mama! Watch my ruffles! They spin with me!" Anika laughs at the delight coming off her daughter in waves.

"Delaney, you look beautiful!"

Dr. Parker and Clara stand to greet her. Anika hugs Clara, who is holding Quinton. "It's lovely to see you both."

Allen fusses a bit as Dr. Parker hands Allen to Daisy. "You look well, Anika. How are you feeling?"

"Better, thank you."

Glenn and his father walk into the room, and Delaney runs straight to the elder Allen. "Mr. Allen, look what Miss Martha made for me!"

"Excuse me, do I know you?" Allen says with a false frown. Delaney giggles and spins for him as he continues teasing her.

Glenn smiles at Delaney, but his smile fades when he looks at Anika. His eyes trace her figure from head to toe, and Anika raises an eyebrow as if daring him.

Martha watches with a cold eye, quietly assessing the family.

Clara turns to Martha, "Would you like to hold the baby?"

"Oh, no, thank you." Martha turns, walking to the fireplace.

"Glenn, I'm sorry for your loss." Mrs. Flannagan rises to take his hand and squeezes them tight.

"Thank you. Will you stay for supper? I'd like to thank you and Miss Martha for coming today." Glenn smiles at Martha, who seems to be talking to Clara.

"Well, we'd love to have a home-cooked meal."

Daisy hands baby Allen to Anika, "I'll check on dinner. Tea is ready, ladies, please help yourself."

"Anika, why don't ya let me hold the little dumpling. You should eat something," Mrs. Flannagan teases her.

Anika laughs and shifts the baby to Mrs. Flannagan, "Thank you. I am hungry all the time."

"That's excellent news, Anika. Just take care that you are drinking enough water. Fluids are extremely important right now," Dr. Parker insists.

"I will, Dr. Parker."

Clara joins her and pours tea, while insisting that Anika put two biscuits with jam on her plate. Delaney happily munches on hers. Anika makes a plate for Martha and walks over to offer it to her while she talks to Glenn.

"Martha, would you care for a plate?"

"Oh, no thank you. I need to watch my figure. Some of us can't afford to eat so much."

Anika's smile falters as she remembers all the times Saul called her fat, sow, heifer, etc. It started off harmless teasing but turned into much worse.

"When you are the lifeline for two other lives, you can afford to eat as much as your body demands. In fact, I insist on it. I want my sons to grow big and strong," Glenn retorts.

Allen laughs, "As if any grandson of mine would have a choice."

Martha is speechless. She glares at Anika, who blushes and walks away to join her daughter. Sitting down, they eat and enjoy tea, while everyone talks.

Dr. Parker waits for Anika to finish eating before bringing up the subject of the contract.

"Glenn, why don't we go over the contract while we wait for supper?" Dr. Parker asks.

"We will watch the boys for you," Clara offers.

"Ladies, excuse us for a few moments." Allen shows Dr. Parker to the library, and Glenn walks over and stops in front of Anika.

"Delaney, can I borrow your Mama for a few minutes?" Delaney looks at her mother and back at Glenn.

"Yes, Mr. Glenn, but you gotta promise to keep her safe."

"I cross my heart, Delaney." He offers his hand to Anika, and she remembers his midnight promise.

Anika grips his hand and is not surprised by the strength she feels. It is warm, sturdy, and comforting just like the man. "Thank you." Glenn tucks her hand in the crook of his arm and guides her from the room.

"Such familiarity," Martha snaps. "For an employee, I mean."

Savannah glares at her brother's retreating back. They will have a serious talk later, but for the moment, this needs to be dealt with. Jealousy and envy are dangerous, and Martha has had her eye on her brother for quite some time.

"Anika is more than an employee. She is a gift. They simply have found each other in similar circumstances, having both lost their spouses," Savannah says quietly.

"Delaney, I have a surprise for you." Clara takes Delaney to look at a doll she brought for her to play with.

"The lass has been through a great deal of trauma, Martha. We will add them to the prayer chain. They need to be lifted up. Glenn seems changed to me." Mrs. Flannagan notes.

"He's angry and hurt. Glenn will need time to heal, and I pray that his walk with the Lord will not be damaged," Savannah murmurs, laying the baby in a wooden cradle.

"It looks like what he needs is a distraction. Perhaps you've all forgotten that we aren't meant to be alone. He needs a young, healthy, wife," Martha snaps.

"Martha! Now is hardly the time for this discussion," Mrs. Flannagan hisses at her.

"Really, if not now, when? I'm only saying what everyone else is saying. He's a war hero and should be treated as such."

Savannah is disgusted with this young woman. She has no idea what they faced in the war. Her beauty truly is only skin deep. "You just tell them to mind their own business, Martha. What he needs is time to heal, not to be set upon by every desperate girl, trying to secure a good match."

"Desperate!" Martha stomps over to grab her wrap, "Mrs. Flannagan, I believe we've overstayed our welcome. You'd do well to remember, Savannah, you're as desperate as the rest of us. Though I'd wager that soiled spinsters like yourself are no threat."

Mrs. Flannagan watches her stomp out of the sitting room and to the front door. "Please forgive her; she's young. Give our excuses to Mr. and Mrs. Ward. You can pick up the dresses next Thursday at my shop." She hands the baby back and sighs before leaving.

Daisy returns to find Savannah murmuring to herself and pacing with the baby in her arms. "Did Mrs. Flannagan just leave?"

Clara returns, just in time to hear Savannah's explanation.

"That girl is disgusting," Clara hisses.

Daisy sighs and sits on the couch. "No, she's only telling the truth. Rumors spread quickly. I'm rather afraid of how Anika and Delaney will be received when we return to church."

"We will just make sure she is surrounded by the Ward family," Savannah snaps. Glenn isn't the only one that can promise to protect their new family members.

Chapter 10

Anika glances around the study and is not surprised to find a room that looks like the man. Dark wood paneling with bookcases full of books. A leather sofa and two sitting chairs flank a large fireplace with a wood coffee table. A large bay window overlooking the back garden has a large mahogany desk with two chairs facing it.

Dr. Parker takes a seat at the couch with the other men opposite her and draws papers out of his black case. He hands one copy to Glenn and one to Anika. "Anika these are the documents we discussed. They detail the arrangement for you to stay on with the Ward family as their nanny for a two-year period. Would you like me to read them to you?"

A soft smile curves her lips as she looks at him. "I can read, Dr. Parker." At his surprised look, she laughs. "I often forget that no one knows me or my history. I was educated by my parents. I can read, paint, sew, play the piano and I can even shoe a horse if I need too."

Allen laughs out loud at that quip, nudging his son. Glenn smiles at her and asks, "Where are you from, Anika?"

Anika takes the papers from Dr. Parker and begins

to scan them, "Virginia." No one moves for a moment, as that bit of news settles between them. "Is that going to be a problem?" Anika asks Glenn.

"Of course not. The war is over, but I wouldn't spread that around. It could cause a lot of trouble for you and Delaney." Glenn explains.

"I understand," she lifts the contract and begins to read.

The first page details the duties of a nanny and live in wet nurse for twin boys. She is to be paid thirty dollars per month for each child. That is sixty dollars a month! Her eyes widen at the number and she glances at Dr. Parker, before glaring at Allen and Glenn. The real caveat is on the last page, where she finds the deed to property, one hundred acres, with a small house for her to do as she wishes.

"Are you serious?" she whispers.

"Is it not enough?" Allen asks softly.

"Not enough?" Anika stares at them incredulously. "This is unthinkable!" She leaps to her feet. "I'll not take your charity. We agreed that I would be hired as a..."

"Charity!" Glenn leaps to his feet, ignoring the warning hand from his father. "You saved my sons lives woman! What price would you put on Delaney's life?"

"Don't you shout at me!" Anika surprises them all by facing Glenn's anger. Turning to the two men, she points to the door. "You need to give us a minute please." Both men look at them and then hurry towards the door.

"Anika are you sure?" Dr. Parker glances uneasily at Glenn. His angry outburst is a shock to him.

"I'll be fine, Glenn won't hurt me, he promised my daughter." Glenn stomps to his desk and pours a glass of whiskey, downing it quickly he savors the way it burns.

"We'll be right outside the door," he says. When the door clicks shut behind them, Glenn spins around to stare at her.

"Anika, you will let me do this for you and Delaney."

"I understand that you feel like you owe me, Glenn, but I owe you just as much. I will accept the pay and the title of Nanny is very generous of you. The land and house are unacceptable. I won't consider it."

"Then you'll not have the job," Glenn snarls and turns back to the desk to pour another whiskey.

Watching him drink in anger is the final straw for her. "I will pack our things and we will leave with Dr. Parker tonight," she snaps.

"You would leave us?" Glenn turns in shock and stops her with his next words. "Anika, I've watched you with my boys. You love them already and its only been four weeks. How can you walk away from them?"

"That's not fair, Glenn." Tears fill her eyes, "I do love them, but did you even think what people will say when you put me up in a house?"

Slowly, he sets the glass down on the desk and walks to the chair to sit down. Running a hand over his tired eyes he sighs heavily. Exhaustion beats at him, and a headache that won't stop.

"To hell, with people, Anika. The house and land are from my parents. It was the original homestead. It needs a lot of work, but I thought with time we could fix it up and I, they want you and Delaney to be taken care of."

"I'm sorry. I do not have the luxury of not caring what people think. I must think of Delaney. I should've asked for clarification before I flew off the handle. Will you forgive me?"

Glenn stares at her, "Does that mean you'll stay?"

"I'll stay, on one condition." She sits in the chair next to him, longing to touch his hand but knowing she can't. "I would ask that you not drink spirits in front of Delaney. It scares her."

"Only her?" His blue eyes stare hard at her, daring her to deny it.

"No," she wrings her hands together in her lap not able to meet his eyes.

"Of course. I have a request of my own. I would ask that you not wear widows' clothes for a man who doesn't deserve it."

Anika's mouth falls open in shock. No one male or female has ever pushed her buttons the way he does.

"You have no right to judge him, Glenn," she hisses and points to the black stripe on his arm, "while you drape your life in the colors of death?"

"He beat you..." Glenn jumps in surprise when she leaps up from her chair.

"Yes, he beat me! He took me away from my family, dishonored our marriage vows and much more, but I wear this for my daughter. To show her that only God gets to judge her father."

"How long?" He glares up at her, ignoring her impassioned speech.

"How long what?" Anika glares at him, tempted to pinch him and her impulse shocks her. Glenn makes her feel that she can say or do anything. Is that a consequence of a growing friendship?

"I'm going to give Sue one more month of my life before I try to find peace and move on. I think Delaney would understand if we had the same time frame, don't you?"

Anika gapes at him, "One month, is all she's worth

to you?"

"Now who's judging, Anika. You think because we have a big house and money that we didn't have problems. It looks like we have a lot to learn about each other." Glenn reaches out and takes her hand, staring at it in awe. "For instance, tell me, how is it that such delicate hands could ever shoe a horse."

Anika freezes, eyes leaping to his and Glenn laughs. She jerks her hand away from his and can't help but laugh with him. Soon he is wiping a tear from his eye that threatens to open a dam in his soul.

"You're right, we do have a lot to learn about each other," she teases and reaches out and tucks his blonde hair behind his ear. Glenn's smile fades and his eyes latch onto hers and her heartbeat accelerates.

Anika drops her hand and walks away, gathering her composure.

"I'll just let them back inside," Glenn says and jumps up quickly and opens the door to allow the men back in the room.

"Do we have an accord?" Dr. Parker asks.

"We do," Anika turns away to sign the documents and Glenn leaves without another word.

"Allen, you and Daisy didn't have to make me such a generous offer, but I'm not stupid enough to refuse it. I thank you for it."

Allen looks out the door and back at her, "No thanks are necessary. Now we can get back to the business of living."

"That sounds nice," Anika says. "Excuse me, I'll go see to the boys."

Dr. Parker waits until she leaves before speaking. "Glenn is headed for trouble, Allen. You need to get him to sleep and not work so many long hours. His anger grows stronger every time I see him."

"I know, I'm not sure what to do about it."

"Perhaps now that the stress is gone, it will abate somewhat."

"We will just have to pray that is true. Let's go eat. I'm starved"

Glenn skips dinner and storms from the house and out to the barn, no longer able to stand the glances of those around him. He knows it was wrong to use the boys to get Anika to agree to stay, but it's what's best for her and the boys. At least that's what he tells himself. Anger fuels his step when he thinks of the predicament they are in. He knows God's plans are not always clear but to bring her into his life now when things are this complicated seems cruel.

"It's best for everyone if we keep our space."

Chapter 11

"Anika, we will walk with you to Mrs. Flannagan's dress shop and then run to the General Store to purchase supplies for the canning we need to do. I have your list of ingredients," Daisy says.

"That sounds complicated. I know my way around town, and her shop is only two doors down," Anika teases.

Allen smiles, "That may be, but you are not alone any longer. Let's compromise. You walk down, and we will pick you up when we're finished."

Anika nods, not trusting herself to speak. They have spoiled her and Delaney. It's hard to believe how her life has changed in five weeks.

"Perfect." Anika glances around the town as she walks away and is shocked how different it seems now. All the shops are connected. From the General store to the post office, courthouse, the town is booming with activity. Main street is busy this time of day, but she is all too aware of the time. Her eyes lock onto the saloon, as men stumble in and out for their lunch break from the Mill.

Anika straightens her plum-colored dress and cropped jacket, thankful for the gloves Savannah gave her this morning, and turns away determined to put that life behind her. Armed with her first paycheck, she is ready to spend some of her money. Today is a day for celebration. They have a large dress order waiting for them, and Delaney is beside herself with joy. She gives a quick wave and hurries to Mrs. Flannagan's Dress Shop.

The bell over the door rings, and Mrs. Flannagan's voice rings out, "Have a look around. I'll be right with ya." Anika grins and takes in the shop. Beautiful bolts of material line tables and hanging on the walls are lovely dresses. The shop is set up in aisles, and Anika begins browsing through determined to find a nightdress to replace her tattered and worn one.

"Ms. Coltrane, how lovely to see ya," Mrs. Flannagan calls out. 'I have your order ready to go, with one exception." She drapes an arm through Anika's and pulls her to the front window. "This sample just came in, and I thought instantly of you, with your coloring." She points to a blue silk taffeta dress, a two-piece button-front fitted bodice with a long tail skirt trimmed in ivory lace.

"It's lovely," Anika gasps and strokes the skirt.

"Yes, it will highlight your eye color and look," she points, "it has a pocket for a watch. Please don't break my heart. Tell me you want it."

"I don't know, Mrs. Flannagan, they've already spoiled me. Let me think about it while you help me with the rest of my purchases." Anika turns away and draws out a small piece of paper and just misses seeing Martha glaring at her through the window.

The shop bell rings again as a new customer enters, and Anika says, "I'm in desperate need of a new nightgown and matching nightdress, Mrs. Flannagan."

"I'll be right back," she points to the back room, "through that door, you will find everything you need.

Mrs. Ward insisted you have what you need, and it will be getting cold soon. You'll even find Delaney's sizes."

Anika smiles and hurries through the door. She is drawn instantly to a baby blue satin nightgown, with its empire waist, and floor length it is stunning. Smiling she runs a finger over the material.

"It's stunning, you should definitely buy it." A voice says, causing her to jump in surprise. Martha is standing in the doorway holding the sample dress from the front window.

"Oh," Anika smiles. "It is exquisite, but I think I need something more practical. Winter is coming." She moves to look at the white cotton gowns with matching wrappers and picks one for herself before looking for Delaney.

"I personally think he would like to see more skin," Martha walks over to a sheer, spaghetti strap, pink, floor-length nightgown and strokes the material. She steps back to eye the matching sheer wrapper and grins at Anika.

"Who?" Anika asks.

"We're all friends here. You don't have to pretend, Anika. I'm sure you've bumped into Glenn at night in that big house of his."

Anika blushes and stares at her in shock. "Excuse me?"

"Everyone is talking about it." She steps closer to Anika, close enough that she can smell her cloying perfume and hisses. "I've waited two years for Glenn to notice me." She grips Anika's upper arm and squeezes, "I don't care what you do or how you dress, Glenn will only ever see you as the hired help or the cow feeding his children. I'll make sure of that. Enjoy your time with him.

It will be fleeting."

Anika jerks her arm away, "Thank you for clarifying that for me, Martha."

Mrs. Flannagan walks in and pauses, "Is there a problem?" She takes in Anika's pale expression and Martha's flushed cheeks and waits.

"No, I would like to buy this." Martha shoves the dress at the older lady and stomps from the room. "Now. I don't have time to dawdle."

"Excuse me, Anika." Mrs. Flannagan hurries after her, and Anika unclenches her hands trying to stop the trembling.

"That creature will not ruin this for me," she tells herself and glances at her note. Everyone is talking about it! Quickly she picks up the underclothes for Delaney and herself, including stockings, two more camisoles built for nursing and petticoats. She is about to pick out a wrapper and gown when Mrs. Flannagan returns.

"I apologize for…"

"No apology needed. Martha's not the first to insinuate disgusting things."

"I see. How are we gettin' on then?" She glances at the boring white cotton gown and sighs. "I have just the thing for ya." On the back wall is a gorgeous white gown and wrapper.

"This is a white cotton nightgown with a square neck for modesty, trimmed with lace and pink silk ribbon, because why not?" she grins. "It buttons from the neckline to the waist, making it perfect for the nursing woman."

Anika smiles but hesitates as Martha's nasty voice runs through her head. "Don't listen to that girl. It's perfect for ya."

"Thank you, I'll take it."

Mrs. Flannagan claps her hands together. "Excellent. Do you need anything else?"

"Denims," Anika grins.

"Ach! Savannah will ruin you yet. I have two pairs, but you will have to try one on."

Anika follows her to the dressing room where an assistant takes her purchases to package them. As soon as she enters the dressing room, Mrs. Flannagan turns to the young assistant, "Get the blue silk nightgown and package it with the matching wrapper. She may never wear it, but neither will Martha."

Daisy enters the shop and finds Anika sipping on tea with Mrs. Flannagan and laughing over something the woman says. "Daisy! You're just in time. We are finished. Though, I just remembered we have some new baby clothes over in the left corner," Mrs. Flannagan hints.

Anika jumps up excitedly, "The boys are outgrowing the dressing gowns. I'll just have a quick look."

Mrs. Flannagan waits till Anika is out of earshot and hisses at Daisy. "Martha was here. I'm not sure what she said to Anika, but it upset her. There is talk in town, Daisy. I thought you should know."

"Thank you." Daisy sighs, "I was afraid of this, and I'm sure it will get worse before it gets better. That girl is desperate to get her claws into Glenn."

"That's true enough, best to make sure someone else does first. If ya get my meaning," she nods her head towards Anika, who squeals over a little boy's suit.

Daisy grins and loops an arm through Mrs. Flannagan. "You're a genius," she whispers.

"Daisy! Look at these! Oh, I hope you have two of them." The ladies laugh and hurry to her side to pick out two cream-colored pants with matching jackets and shirts. Before they leave, they add two chocolate velvet pantsuits and hats.

Chapter 12

Allen waits out front with the wagon, and they're quickly loaded up. Anika reaches into the back and grabs her carpet bag before stepping to Allen and Daisy, who are saying goodbye to Mrs. Flannagan.

"Allen, I need to make one stop before we go home if that's alright?" she asks softly.

"Of course, name it," he offers a hand to his wife to assist her into the wagon.

"I need to stop at the Charity Home for Orphans. I have a few quilts to drop off."

Daisy glances down at her bag and smiles. "I thought they were for Delaney?"

"No, these are specially sized for the children. Two by four feet, sometimes longer for the older children. It's only three this time. I've been really busy."

"Daisy, it's been too long since we've had a Quilting Bee. What better project than the children?" Mrs. Flannagan gasps, "I have tons of scrap pieces of material that we can use."

"That's a wonderful idea! Anika, what do you think?"

"I think you're both amazing. The children have nothing, and there are one hundred thirty-four children at this one home." All three people stop moving and stare at her in shock.

"How could we not know this, Allen?" Daisy gasps.

"I don't know, but we will bring this up at church on Sunday. Let's go visit and see what else they need," Allen replies with a determined glint.

Anika hugs Mrs. Flannagan and climbs into the wagon, hoping she didn't upset them. Three blocks down the street, they turn, and Anika points to a large brick three-story building. It's vacated due to shell damage after the war.

Allen handles the horses with practiced ease, offering a reassuring smile to Anika. The wagon sets off, the rhythmic clatter of hooves against the cobblestone streets accompanied by the gentle creaking of the wooden carriage.

"There it is. It has been repaired by some of the Mill workers. I usually just drop the quilts with Pastor Donegal. He runs the children's home."

"Perfect. Let's go see him," Allen replies, leading the way. Anika follows, the ladies beside her, and they enter the dark doorway of the orphanage. The anticipation of a somber interior fills the air.

To Allen's surprise, the inside is warmly lit, revealing a welcoming entryway adorned with rugs and a large fireplace. Comfortable chairs and couches are thoughtfully arranged, creating multiple seating areas for various purposes. The atmosphere is unexpectedly cozy, dispelling any preconceived notions of a gloomy orphanage.

Pastor Donegal, a kindly figure with greying hair and a gentle smile, walks towards them with a handsome man at his side. The warmth in his eyes welcomes them the moment they step inside the orphanage. "Ms.

Coltrane, welcome back. Mr. and Mrs. Ward, it's nice to see you. You remember Rhemi Darlington."

"Of course, hello Mr. Darlington," Daisy says with genuine politeness. Rhemi bows slightly, a gesture of refinement, and smiles at Anika.

"I don't think I've had the pleasure." His well-manicured hand extends toward her, causing Anika to instinctively step back.

"Excuse me, Mr. Darlington, this is Anika Coltrane, our new nanny," Allen introduces her, keenly observing the flicker of interest in Rhemi's eyes.

"Rhemi just made a generous donation to the Orphan's home, and we are ever so grateful. The Darlington family owns the Mill and has generously offered to pay for the repairs to the building," Pastor Donegal explains.

"That's very kind of you," Anika replies diplomatically, appreciating the charitable efforts.

"Perhaps I could arrange a tour of the Mill for you, Ms. Coltrane." Rhemi steps closer, a seemingly innocent suggestion, "I have a new covered carriage that is sure to keep out the evening chill."

Daisy's eyes narrow at the audacity of the suggestion, and Allen feels her stiffen in outrage beside him. Trying to diffuse the tension, Allen interjects, "Is that your new carriage out front? I saw a group of men looking it over. She sure is a beauty."

Rhemi's eyes snap to his, and he stammers a quick goodbye, perhaps sensing the shift in the atmosphere. Daisy nudges Allen and shares a smile with the Pastor. Anika grins, silently observing Rhemi's hasty exit, her thoughts involuntarily comparing him to Glenn.

Rhemi, dressed in the finest navy day suit

with perfectly combed hair, clearly emanates affluence. However, he seems too pristine for Anika's taste. She prefers a man who carries the natural scent of hard work and the outdoors.

"What can I do for you folks?" Pastor Donegal's voice interrupts her musings.

An hour later, as they sit in the wagon, a heavy silence hangs in the air. Daisy reaches for Allen's hands, expressing the shock at the conditions of the orphanage.

"How could we be so blind? They don't even have beds!" Allen snaps the reins, urging the horses to hurry home.

"They are the lucky ones," Anika explains calmly. Daisy and Allen stare at her in horror.

"Why would you say that?" Daisy asks, bewildered.

"Some sleep inside doorways, under bridges, wherever they can find shelter. They go days without eating. It must be dealt with, or they will turn to crime and other means of survival," Anika clarifies, offering a stark reality check.

"Sunday is going to be eye-opening for our congregation," Allen states, determined to address the issue.

"You will go with us, Anika, and I'm going to suggest the proceeds from our bake sale go to this charity and organize a quilting bee."

"I, I don't know if I'm ready, Daisy."

"It's much easier to gossip about someone you don't know, Anika. Once they see you with our family, things will die down."

Allen listens quietly as they ride through town, contemplating the newfound awareness that has gripped them.

Anika hurries to the nursery upon their return and finds both boys being changed by the new help, Mrs. Henrietta, a sixty-year-old freed slave, whom Glenn insisted on hiring for this role.

"How did they do?" Anika asks as she picks up Allen.

"Just fine, though they are about to start fussing. You want me to stay and help?" Mrs. Henrietta asks.

"No, ma'am. Thank you for coming today. It was nice to get out."

"My pleasure. When do you need me next?" she asks.

"Can you come Monday? I would like to help with the canning and cooking?"

"Of course. I'll be here at eight."

Anika hums and rocks Allen, stroking his dark head. Savannah knocks softly and moves to the cradle to look at Quinton.

"He's starting to get fussy." She picks him up and places his cheek to hers while Anika watches.

"Will you switch with me?" They switch babies, and she holds Allen and touches his cheek.

"Savannah, what can you tell me about Martha?"

"Martha is ... what's the Christian way to say it, a busybody, trouble; she sews discord wherever she goes." Savannah blushes when she looks at Anika.

"She hurt you," Anika states, and it's not a question.

"I thought she did, but she merely saved me from a bad situation. Once I was to be married, but when he found out I aspired to be a photographer, he changed his mind."

Anika listens quietly as she rocks and waits for her to talk.

"Anika, could I borrow the homestead for a little while?" Savannah asks unexpectedly.

"Of course," she replies.

"Aren't you going to ask me why?" Savannah asks.

"No. Your reasons are your own, and I've no need of the homestead yet." She lifts Quinton to her shoulder to burp him and smiles at her new friend. "Can I help with anything?"

"Thank you. I would love the help, and I'm not sure others would understand."

"I will help you in any way I can. Dr. Parker says I should start walking. I'll have Ms. Henrietta come, and we can start Friday."

"Perfect. I just need to get it cleaned up. Why don't we get these two changed and go eat; I'm starved."

"You read my mind, and Savannah, if you ever need to talk, I'm here."

Savannah looks at her and smiles softly, "Thank you, Anika. I'm glad you're here."

"Me too."

Chapter 13

Anika's hands tremble as she cautiously descends from the wagon. It's the first Sunday back at church since Sue's passing, and it marks Delaney's inaugural Sunday as an official member of the family. Delaney, adorned in her new dress, radiates excitement. Allen extends a helping hand to Daisy first and then Delaney, while Savannah, ever spontaneous, jumps down before anyone can assist her. Daisy gracefully takes one baby from Anika, and Allen, in sync with Glenn, lifts the other. Glenn descends and turns to help Anika down. His hands encircle her slender waist, and he smiles as he gently lowers her to the ground.

"You look lovely in purple, Ms. Coltrane," he compliments.

"Thank you," Anika forces a smile, and Glenn holds onto her waist until she meets his gaze.

"Glenn?" Her eyes flicker with a warning.

"That's more like it. I like to see the fire in your eyes, not fear. I told you that you had nothing to fear with us, and I meant it." He releases her waist and turns to assist his mother with the baby.

Observing from the back of the wagon, Allen hurries to Anika, diverting her attention. "He's fussing."

Anika takes the baby, patting him gently as she walks, escorted by Allen to the front of the Church. Pastor Donegal and his wife Beatrice warmly greet the church members at the entrance. "Welcome back, Glenn."

"Oh, let's see the boys!" Beatrice calls, and soon all the women surround the babies, eager to meet Anika. Daisy handles introductions while Delaney is led to Sunday school. Delaney glances back at Anika, hesitating to let go, but a little girl runs up, taking her hand and guiding her inside the small room. A smile breaks across Delaney's face, accompanied by giggles.

Relieved, Anika smiles. Savannah leads her to a pew at the front of the church, with Glenn and Allen standing on either side. Anika prays silently that both babies make it through the service. Surprisingly, Daisy and Savannah settle on her right side, while Glenn takes his place on her left. Glenn smiles down at baby Quinton, touching his dark head.

"Let's hope they stay asleep," he whispers in her ear.

Pastor Donegal smiles at the congregation before commencing his sermon. "Good Morning, today we are glad to welcome back the Ward family. Our prayers have been with you all, and if ever there was a time to believe in miracles, it is now."

"Mr. Ward has asked that we baptize the boys this morning. If you would all be patient while they bring both boys to us."

Anika jerks in surprise, attempting to hand over Quinton, but Glenn pulls her to her feet. "Not without you," he whispers. Daisy hands over baby Allen, and they guide her forward.

Trying not to cause a scene, she walks to the pulpit. "Glenn, you stand here on the left and hold him." He smiles at Anika and explains, "I will do this while you each hold a baby."

His wife holds the bowl of water as he dips a cloth and squeezes it over the dark newborn head. Quinton fusses a bit, but soon settles, eliciting quiet laughter from the congregation.

"Heavenly Father, in your love you have called us to know you, led us to trust you, and bound our life with yours. Surround these boys with your love, protect them from evil. Fill them with the Holy Spirit and receive them into the family of your church. Show them how to walk in the way of Christ and grow in faith and love. Amen."

Pastor Donegal takes Quinton, and his wife takes Allen. They turn to the congregation and walk through the aisles. "We welcome to our church, Quinton and Allen Ward." His voice booms out, "Will you protect them, love them, and guide them?"

"We will!" The congregation responds in unison.

Glenn draws Anika close, feeling her trembling. She smiles up at him and wipes a tear. He looks so proud in that moment. "Thank you," she hears him say softly.

Anika smiles out at the congregation, and her smile fades a little when she notices Martha glaring at her. Martha nudges a friend and whispers in her ear, grinning. Thankfully, the service is short, and when the boys start to fuss, they make excuses and collect Delaney. Daisy is quick to spread the word about the quilting bee while Anika walks Delaney to the wagon.

"Mama, I made new friends!" Delaney is glowing with excitement.

"I'm so proud of you, Delaney." She smiles as Allen lifts her into the wagon.

"It was fun, Mama, and they prayed for Daddy and

Rosie." Anika jerks as if slapped.

"What?" she whispers.

Delaney walks to the edge of the wagon and cups Anika's face in her hands. "Don't be mad, Mama. Mrs. B said I can talk to them when I miss them by praying, and then they prayed with me." Tears flood her eyes.

"Of course, I'm not mad at you, Delaney. You pray anytime you want to."

Delaney throws her arm around her neck. "Thank you, Mama."

"You're welcome. Now let's go home."

Glenn is walking back from the front of the church when he hears his name called. "You lucked out, didn't you, Ward."

George, Albert, and Rhemi are standing together, staring at Anika as Allen helps her climb into the wagon, followed by his sister, Savannah.

"What does that mean?" his glare should be warning enough, but part of him hopes they step out of line.

"Only that your new nanny is luscious," Albert says, leering at her.

Glenn grabs Albert by the front of his pressed shirt before he can finish his lewd statement.

"The question you should ask is how lucky do you feel right now?" Glenn growls.

Pastor Donegal interrupts with a frown and steps between them. He pries Glenn's hand free and pushes the three men back.

"None of that now, Glenn, your family is waiting for you. Let's not mar this beautiful day with violence."

"I didn't mean anything by it, Glenn," Albert stammers.

"I think you meant exactly what you said!" Glenn tries to grab him again only to be pushed back by the Pastor. "Having just buried the mother of my children I don't exactly feel lucky. You should be thankful we are in God's house. Keep your eyes and your vulgar comments to yourself. Next time, I won't be so restrained."

Glenn storms back to the wagon. He doesn't trust himself to speak.

"What was that about?" Daisy asks.

"Nothing," he replies shortly.

Chapter 14

"I've never canned so much in my life," Anika says with a satisfied grin.

"Applesauce, apple butter, cherry preserves, peaches, and more. We did great. I couldn't have gotten this done without both of you," Daisy smiles at them and watches Savannah stack the last of the mason jars into the tray.

"Perfect. We have earned a few days off before we start baking for the bake sale. It's all everyone is talking about at church," Savannah says with a grin.

"I'm really pleased to see how everybody has stepped up to help, and all the proceeds are going to the Orphans' Home," Daisy replies.

"I am excited to see how well the raffle works," Anika says.

"The finished quilt is stunning, Anika. It will be fun to see how much money it raises," Daisy yawns.

"Thanks to your sewing machine, it went together much faster than I had hoped," Anika says. "It will make the smaller quilts easier to make as well."

"The Quilting Bee is going to be the social event of the year! Just wait, Savannah, so much food, and laughter."

"Until the men show up," Daisy teases.

"It will be great fun, and Anika can meet all the church members in a more informal setting," Savannah glances at her mother. "Mama, you look tired. Why don't you go get cleaned up, Anika and I will put these in the root cellar," Savannah insists.

"Okay, I am a mess." She wipes her hands on a stained apron and hurries from the room. Savannah glances out the window behind her mother and smothers a grin of delight when she sees her brother, Glenn walking from the barn towards the back door. These two could use some time together, she thinks. They have avoided each other since the incident at church.

"I'll get the first tray while you fill the other one." Savannah grabs a wooden tray and carefully pushes through the door, walking across the yard, through the garden, and towards the cellar door. The fresh autumn wind blows across the yard, and Savannah smiles at Glenn.

"Need help?" Glenn asks when he looks up and notices his sister struggling with a heavy wooden tray.

"What a great brother. Could you take this to the root cellar?"

Glenn pushes his wide-brimmed hat back on his head and takes the tray. "Why do I feel like I'm being duped? Did you plan it this way?"

"Why, whatever do you mean, brother?" She bats her long lashes and giggles when he glowers and heads to the cellar beside the barn. It is a heavy trap door, leading down into an eight by ten-foot, limestone-lined cellar. It stays a cool fifty-two degrees year-round.

Glenn descends into the darkened space, careful not to hit his head on the low ceiling. The sun is setting, and it's getting dark, so he drops the tray on a shelf and moves to the right side where he knows the lantern is kept. He stoops down to dig around for a match.

Savannah passes Anika as she walks towards the cellar door. "I left it open for you. I'm going to grab a bath. Mom has the boys so don't fret about them." She hurries past Anika and ducks behind the wagon to wait for her opportunity.

Anika frowns but is preoccupied with the trap door. Built into the ground, it looms ahead, taunting her. She takes a deep breath, "You can do this," she murmurs as she starts down the stone steps, carrying a wooden tray full of rattling glass jars. The scent of damp earth strikes her nose, and she frowns at the dark interior. Her heart beats harder with each step she takes.

"It's just a cellar, Anika," she tells herself, but why does it feel like stepping into a nightmare. Her hands are sweaty and shaking, and she tells herself, "Just drop it and go." She places the tray on the closest shelf and turns to leave.

"Need help?" Glenn smothers a laugh when she screams in terror. Her large blue eyes are wide, and she whirls in a panic to run. The door slams shut above them, casting them into total darkness.

Savannah slams the door, ignoring the startled scream from below, and slides the lock into place. She whistles and walks back to the house. One cup of coffee should be enough time, or maybe two? These two people need a little push in the right direction. What harm could come from giving them a little alone time? She is chuckling as she walks up the back steps into the kitchen.

"Damn!" Glenn snarls and places the lantern on the nearest stone ledge. It creates a soft glow. "Don't move, let your eyes adjust."

"No, no, no," Anika mumbles and turns, looking past him for an escape. "Not again, no..." she moans and runs her hands along the wall, looking for a way out. Panic flows in, and she is gasping for breath.

"Anika, look at me. You're safe here." He reaches for her only to leap back when she shouts at him.

"No! I can't breathe!" She tries to run back up the steps and push on the door, but it is too heavy. "Oh, God!" She lifts her skirt and runs down the steps, gasping for breath.

"It's okay, Savannah is just playing a trick on us. You're safe." Glenn approaches her slowly, like a wounded animal, only to stop moving when she backs away from him shaking her head in terror. When her hand goes to her throat, he realizes that she's in a full panic.

"I can open it," he runs up the steps and pushes hard, but it is latched shut. "No!" He shouts for help, praying someone will hear him. Most of the pickers have left for the day, and his father is already at home. The sounds coming from Anika terrify him.

When he turns, she is looking around desperately for a way out. Her hands are running along the walls, pushing at the limestone blocks, praying for an escape, and begging someone to help her. "Please, oh... please, let me out, not again..."

Glenn corners her in the back of the cellar. "Stop!" He shouts. Anika pushes back against the cold stones and sees a large, looming, dark shadow of a man. "It's Glenn. You know me. I would never hurt you," he calls to her softly.

"Anika, I'm here. See me," he whispers, and steps towards her. One hand reaches out, and she steps towards him. "That's right, you aren't alone." Tears stream down her face, and she seems to understand for the first time.

"Glenn?"

"Yes, come here," he pleads, and she rushes into his open arms and sobs.

"Don't let go," she begs. Anika balls her hands into his shirt and holds on for dear life. In that moment, she doesn't care about propriety, only that he is holding her, and it feels like heaven.

"Not a chance." Finally, his soul shouts, she is where she belongs. When she looks up at him, he wipes her tears away with his thumbs, and she is lost.

"Glenn..." she whispers and drags his mouth to hers, knocking his hat to the dirt floor. Neither resists the pull, as if they could. He kisses her as if his life depends on it, deep, ravenous, hot, and intense, and she is swept away. Glenn lifts her against his body and spins, pressing her against the cold limestone walls.

All her panic is forgotten as her body responds to his touch. He groans and rips his mouth away from hers. Anika stares at him in total shock, intending to apologize but he isn't ready just yet to let her go. This time his mouth takes her slowly.

"Anika, you taste like Heaven," he murmurs as his tongue traces her lips. Moist heat, hot and heady, flows through them, and she buries a hand in his long hair, praying he never lets her go. She kisses him back, memorizing the flavor that is his and groans when he pulls away.

"Are you guys okay?" Savannah calls and struggles with the weight of the door.

Glenn slides her to the ground and takes a deep breath. He grabs her hand, pulling her along behind him.

"It's jammed, Savannah..." he starts to say, but she has managed to pry it open, allowing light to flood in. His eyes narrow in fury.

"I'm so sorry, it must have blown shut."

Glenn drops Anika's hand and stomps up the steps, causing his sister to back away from him.

"Our lives are not some game for you to play with, Savannah!" he rumbles in a low voice.

Savannah takes another step back from her brother. "I didn't mean to cause trouble, Glenn."

"I think you meant to do exactly what you did. Mind your own business from now on." Glenn leaves without looking back, and Anika has yet to emerge from the cellar. Slowly she ascends, one step at a time, and when Savannah sees her, she gasps. The tracks of her tears can't be erased, but the haunted look in her eyes is heart-breaking.

"Anika, are you okay?"

"I, I don't like enclosed spaces."

Savannah hugs her and guides her to the steps. "Oh, let's get you inside."

After the children have been fed and tucked in, Anika walks out to the side porch. It has a swing which she loves to relax in. Tonight, she desperately needs to be outside. The blanket she carries should keep her warm enough, that and the thought of his kiss. Her attraction to Glenn has only grown stronger with the passing of time. It's only been a few months, she tells herself. They barely know each other, and she is wishing for things she shouldn't wish for.

Glenn watches her walk past his study and decides to follow her. Anika walks into the small porch and draws the blanket around her shoulders.

"Can I join you?"

Anika jumps at the sound of his deep voice. "Of course, it's your home." She sits and swings softly, laying her head back on the wooden swing. It creaks beneath his weight, and instantly she wishes she'd said no. The heat radiating from his body is tempting, and she struggles with how to talk to him. They swing in silence for a moment before she draws in a deep breath and gets her speech over with.

"Glenn, I owe you an apology for today. I was way out of line, and if you wish to find someone else to care for the boys, I will understand."

Glenn stops swinging and turns to look at her in complete surprise. "What are you apologizing for?"

"You know why," she hisses.

"Anika, it was just a kiss," he runs a hand over his face while she interrupts.

"Two kisses."

"Exactly," two amazing kisses he thinks. "The point is that you were upset, and I was trying to distract you." The lie falls easily from his lips, and she stares at him in embarrassment.

"Distract me?" Shame has her head dropping, "That is one way to do it, I suppose," she murmurs. "I'm sorry you had to witness my break down." Anika stands and wraps the blanket protectively around herself. "I'm embarrassed. Saul thought it was funny to torment me in varied ways." Images flash, running through her mind, and she closes her eyes against the onslaught. "Sometimes he would lock me in closets if I was lucky."

"If you weren't lucky, what did he do?" Glenn asks gruffly.

"Games, he called them." Her eyes open, and she

glances at the dark land in front of her, not able to bring herself to meet his stare. "It doesn't matter, does it? He's dead, and I'm free of him... I thought I was free, but I think that maybe I'm still broken."

A Bible verse strikes his heart strong, and he is surprised by it. "God can restore what is broken and change it into something amazing. All you need is faith." He quotes the verse given to him from Joel 2:25.

Anika stares at him in surprise. "I hope so, Glenn."

Glenn stands up and forces himself to leave her, stopping at the door, he glances back at her. "I'm broken too, Anika." He takes a deep breath and gives her the truth she deserves. "This shared attraction between us can't go anywhere. I can't give you what I wish I could. It wouldn't be fair to any of us. You deserve a whole man, not a shell of one." He leaves her staring after him in confusion.

Chapter 15

"This is going to be the best harvest we've had in some time," Allen boasts proudly.

"I should hope so, you all have been working nonstop these last six weeks. Did the last shipment make it out on time?" Daisy asks, handing him a fresh cup of black coffee.

"It did. Glenn's suggestion of using this new Rivers refrigerated shipping method was genius," Allen tries to steal a cookie only to have his hand slapped.

Anika laughs at the sad look on Allen's face. "Don't give me that look, Allen Ward these are for the bake sale. As well as those two pies cooling on the table."

"Don't worry, Allen, I'm taking over the kitchen tonight and I promise to save some treats for you," Anika says.

"I knew I liked you." Allen steals a kiss from his wife and swipes a cookie from the unprotected side with a laugh.

Anika giggles, drawing a contented smile from Daisy. Her health has rebounded, and the color has returned to her cheeks. "Is Glenn still working?" Anika asks as she begins gathering her supplies for the deserts she'll be making.

"He is. Hopefully, now that picking season is slowing down he will rest." Allen says with a worried glance at his wife. "I'm sorry you've had to post pone the bake sale and quilting bee until after Harvest but now that we have finished up we should have a great turn out."

"October is my favorite time of year." Daisy turns to Allen, "This apple harvest has been amazing, and we finished early. Once we get through the bake sale and Quilting bee we can enjoy the holidays with our family." Daisy grips her husband's arm.

"The boys are sleeping, and Delaney is down for the night. Why don't you two go spend some time together?" Anika suggests.

"I think she wants the kitchen to herself, wife."

"No, it's just that..."

"He's teasing you, Anika. I could use a rest if I'm honest." Daisy stifles a yawn and takes her husband's hand. Before she gets to the door, she turns, "Savannah is listening for the boys, while she works in her room. She'll come get you if you are needed. Enjoy the quiet."

"Thank you." Envy fills her heart as she watches them leave together. Three months spent with them has taught her that the love they share runs deep, and they are well suited. Her parents loved each other too. She is so thankful that Delaney gets to see this kind of love in action. It's a surprise to find that she longs for that companionship and love. Glenn's face pops in her mind, but she pushes that secret desire away, he made it more than clear that he isn't interested.

The first dough needs to be refrigerated overnight before rolling out. All three batches were made last night, tonight she is assembling and baking.

"Which first?" She chews her lip as she thinks

aloud. "The open tarts are the quickest to make." She mixes the dough and then grabs a large bowl and begins peeling and slicing plums and apples. Once that is complete she rolls out the pie crusts flat and slices it into small hand-held sized portions. She tops each with plums, or apples, being careful to keep the fruit in the center. A quick egg wash and she rolled the edges up around to form the tarts crusty edges. Anika is elated to find that one batch of dough will make two dozen small tarts. She slides them in the hot oven and returns to the counter.

"That means I will have four dozen German Tarts?"

"Sounds delicious." Glenn almost laughs when she startles and whirls around, until he sees the fear on her face.

"Damnit, I didn't mean to frighten you, Anika." He steps towards her and she laughs nervously.

"I didn't hear you come in," she glances at him and is shocked by his gaunt appearance. A thick, full, beard covers his face and shaggy hair, but it is the haunted expression in his eyes that cause her to pause.

"We saved you a plate, sit down and I'll get it for you."

Glenn stares at her retreating back, "Something smells amazing, please tell me that I get to be your taste tester?"

"We'll see," she teases softly, "but first you have the finish your dinner." Anika places a big bowl of Brunswick stew in front of him and a dinner roll. "Coffee?"

"Thank you," he avoids further eye contact with her and digs into his soup.

Anika pulls the first patch of pastries from the oven and slides the second one in before turning to begin working on the German tarts. The kitchen fills with the scent of baked pies and Glenn sits back to sip his coffee and watch her work.

While the first batch cools, she grabs the dough from the ice box and begins the process of rolling it and slicing. Each is sliced into long strips about six inches long.

"I haven't seen you lately, how are you?" He asks.

"I'm doing well. I must thank you for hiring Mrs. Henrietta, she's a dream come true. It gives me time with Delaney and the boys love her."

"I'm glad to hear it."

"How are you?" She asks as she dusts the table with flour and sits to begin the long process of twisting each strip. Once they are twisted she swirls them in a circle and places them on the baking sheet.

"Tired." He sips his coffee and steals a tart from the cookie sheet.

"Hey," she laughs as he smirks.

"But not too tired to swipe one of these."

"It's not finished yet, I will dust them with the glaze just before serving."

"Don't mess with perfection, Anika," he says taking a huge bite.

They stare at each other before she breaks away with a stammer, "They won't be perfect if I burn them." She hurries to the oven to pull the second batch out.

Glenn notices everything about her, from the healthy sheen to her hair, to the blush on her cheeks and even the smooth way she moves. Her wounds have healed well. Anika is a beautiful woman and he's has been purposely avoiding her. The first three weeks he spent a great deal of his nights with her and the twins, but it only made his attraction towards her grow stronger. After the cellar incident he stopped them all together. He doesn't trust himself to be alone with her and not touch her.

"I've missed you," he murmurs.

Anika freezes and her eyes jump to his. They both jump when Savanna walks into the kitchen holding a fussing baby. "Look who woke up."

Glenn smiles and reaches for his son. He calms as soon as he's lifted to his chest.

"He smelled the amazing pastries, no doubt," Glenn says.

"Pastries? Anika, please tell me I can have one," Savannah pleads.

"Okay, but only if you promise to walk with me tomorrow." Glenn's eyebrows lift in surprise.

"Deal," she chooses her tart and sits at the table.

"Walk with you where?" He grumbles and pats his son.

"To the homestead, we've been cleaning it out for the past few weeks," Anika replies and carefully applies a teaspoon of jam to the center of each cookie sized pastry.

Savannah watches the expressions on Glenn's face carefully. "Let me do that and you start the next batch," she offers.

"Thank you, Savannah. I thought I'd have more time before they woke, but Quinton has decided to play catch up with his brother. He's getting so big."

"Why?" Glenn demands louder this time and pats his sons back causing a large burp.

"Wow, he sounds just like you, Daddy." Savannah attempts to lighten the moment.

"Why what?" Anika quips ignoring Savannah as she slides another pan in the oven.

Glenn glares, "Why are you working at the homestead, you have two years before that is an issue."

"One year and nine months, actually." Anika stands up and stretches before grabbing her dusting sugar to top the first pan of cooled pastries.

"So, your counting down to when you can leave us?" Glenn snaps.

Anika stops moving and turns to glare at him.

"You can't have it both ways. You've made your position clear, Mr. Ward."

"Don't be ridiculous," Glenn barks.

"Ridiculous," she hisses. Anika slaps the canister on the table and faces a startled pair of eyes, Ignoring Savannah, she snaps, "First you try to decide what I need in a man and now I'm ridiculous!"

"There is no need for you to be working on the homestead. Why are you so dead set on working out there?"

"Well, Mr. Ward, I happen to need the exercise, I enjoy the sunshine and because I want to. Why are you being such a bully?"

"Bully? I merely asked a question. You shouldn't be working there alone."

"Who said I was alone?" Glenn's mouth drops open in surprise.

Savannah smothers a smile and reaches for a sleepy baby, "I'll just lay him back down." She hurries from the kitchen.

They ignore her as they face off. "Who have you been seeing?"

"That's not the point, Mr. Ward." He steps closer to her and is quietly pleased that she doesn't back away from him.

"Dr. Parker cleared me weeks ago to return to regular activities. Which you would know if you were around more. I've been helping your sister."

"It's not safe for you to be traipsing all over the countryside unescorted, Dr. Parker would agree with me."

Anika pokes his chest and snaps, "Maybe you should see him Glenn. It looks like you are working yourself thin."

Glenn grabs her hand and they both stop moving. "Did you just poke me?"

Anika's lips curl into a small smile, "Yes, I did."

The trust she shows humbles him. 'I've missed you,' he thinks and almost says it out loud, again.

"You've been avoiding me," Anika murmurs and pulls her hand away. Turning away from him, he catches a glimpse of the hurt. She grabs a bowl and mixes a glaze of sugar, vanilla, and juice. Glenn moves so close behind her that she can feel the heat of his body warming hers. The pounding of his heart is thumping in his ears and he struggles with the need to touch her. Her bravery and kindness pull at him.

"It's better this way," Glenn murmurs and leaves swiftly before he fails them both.

"Better for whom?" Anika doesn't turn to watch him go, she continues working until the final pastries are baked. Two hours later after cleaning the kitchen, she finds her way to the nursery.

Widows remarry often and as quickly as possible, but she is not in the same class as the Ward family, she reminds herself. He was right about one thing, they are both broken, but she refuses to live the rest of her life in fear. With the pastor's guidance she has been studying her bible and attempting to heal.

Anika set the lantern down on the dresser and steps over to the walnut crib, expecting to find both boys asleep. Quinton is staring at her and the moment she smiles at him, he grins and starts kicking his feet.

"Hi, little man," her eyes fill with tears as she picks him up and cuddles him to her. Images of Rosie fills her mind and heart. She lets the tears flow freely as sits in the rocker to nurse him. Her tears don't seem to want to stop. Quinton sleeps as she places him gently back in his bed and repairs her dress. Moving to the window Anika stares out into the star filled night, October is almost over, and the cold is a welcome relief. She wipes at her tear stained cheeks and takes a deep breath, sleep will not come easy this night.

Glenn steps inside intending to apologize but finds Anika in tears. "What's wrong?" He demands and hurries to her side.

"If you've come to shout at me, don't." She turns her face away from him and sits on the window seat.

Glenn squats down next to her, "Talk to me."

"Rosie," the word is laced with love and pain. Glenn bows his head to her knees as if unable to bear the sound of her name.

Anika touches his hair, running her fingers over his head and neck. Glenn looks up at her and grabs her hand gently. "Glenn, in my mind's eye, I can imagine all her firsts. Her first smile, her first laugh, even her first fit and it torments me."

"I understand."

Anika glances quickly away from him. "How could you possibly understand. God blessed you with two healthy sons."

Glenn stands up quickly and stares at her.

"I'm sorry, I shouldn't have said that" she whispers swiping at her tears.

"Don't be sorry, you're right. I wish I could help you." His anger boils at the thought of her in pain. "It shouldn't be this way."

"You help me every day, Glenn. I'm not sure I could find a better listener."

"At least I can do that." He sighs and stands up to leave, but her words stop him.

"You've done more than that, Glenn. You've given us a safe place to call home, restored my dreams and been a friend when I needed one. Don't take my tears for weakness. I miss my daughter, but when I hold your sons they make the pain more bearable." She steps to the crib and looks down at them. Glenn joins her and smiles down at the identical dark-haired babies.

"Allen rolled over today, and Quinton is right with him." Pride has her laughing softly, before looking up at him. "Is it wrong to love them so quickly?" She whispers.

Glenn drapes an arm around her shoulder and tugs her into his side. "No, they need your love," and so do I, his heart says.

He presses a kiss to the side of her head and leaves quickly. "Good night, Anika."

His anger pulses through his body forcing him from the farmhouse and into the barn. The nightmares won't leave him be. Last night Sue was holding the babies and running away from him, through a bloody field of dead soldiers. A severed hand grabbed her foot tripping her and she fell screaming and tossing the babies in the air. He woke up shouting and covered in sweat. Glenn stomps through night to the empty barn stall where he begins punching on a curved wall that has seen too much blood and fury. Anika is a temptation that is driving him to distraction. Guilt at having lost his wife and anger at his circumstances eat at his soul.

Savannah follows her brother into the barn and watches in horrified silence as he beats out his rage. When his blood begins to cover the wall, she steps behind him.

"What in God's name are you doing?"

Glenn stops beating the wall but doesn't turn around, his head drops, "Go away, Savannah, you wouldn't understand."

Savannah ignores him and grabs a clean towel from a cabinet in the cold barn. "Anika didn't tell you the truth, about the homestead."

His head snaps up at that bit of information. "What are you talking about?" She gently wraps one hand and then the other, only to flinch when he hisses in pain.

"She wasn't alone at the homestead." His eyes fly open wide and he glares at her. Savannah chuckles, "That's what I thought. You two have feelings for each other, but she deserves better than this display and so do you."

"My feelings don't matter." Glenn jerks his hand away and snaps, "You wouldn't understand."

"I understand more than you think. Sometime soon, you and I will take a ride and I'll show you what she's been up to." She stomps out of the barn and prays that this the right thing to do.

Chapter 16

Anika gently grasps Delaney's hand, excitement lighting up her face. "I've never worked a bake sale before. This should be fun, right Delaney?" In her other hand, she carries a carpet bag. Glenn walks beside them, wooden box of pastries in hand, listening to their conversation.

Delaney shrugs, her shoulders slumping. "I guess."

Anika looks at her in surprise. "That doesn't sound like my girl. What's wrong?"

"I don't know," Delaney mumbles.

"Delaney, did you know that we'll be joined at the sale by some of the church families, including boys and girls your age?" Glenn explains.

"That's nice, Mr. Ward."

Anika glances down at Delaney and squeezes her hand gently. "Clara will be there, and you look so pretty in your new dress. Today is a chance to make new happy memories, Delaney."

Delaney stops walking, surprising them both. "Mama, when we're done, can we go see them?"

Anika stoops down to eye level with her daughter. "See who?"

"Daddy and Rosie," she whispers.

All color drains from Anika's face. "Oh sweetie, of

course we can."

Delaney throws her arms around Anika and wipes her eyes. "Thank you, Mama."

"I'd do anything for you, Delaney."

Delaney skips to catch up with Savannah, and Glenn stares at her, struggling to compose himself. "You're one hell of a woman, Anika Coltrane."

Anika blushes and smiles. "Thank you." She hurries to catch up to her daughter, putting some distance between them. It's better if they aren't seen together. Delaney needs to find peace, and Anika will do whatever it takes to help her, even if it means visiting the cemetery.

Today is an important step in reclaiming her life. Joining the Ward family at church will give them a fresh start. Delaney needs to meet children her own age. Anika straightens her blue velvet dress and matching overcoat, wondering how the other church members will react to her. Many young women are without husbands or are widowed with children. It's best if she isn't seen as a threat to them. The money from the bake sale goes to help the widows and orphans from the war. Unfortunately, too many are still struggling with daily needs like food and shelter.

First Baptist Church is beautiful from the outside —a unique all-brick building with a steeply pitched roof and a simple red brick facade that accentuates the pointed, arched stained glass windows. The tall, thin spires draw the eye to the crowning glory—the bell house surrounded by the spires, with its large cast bronze bell gleaming in the morning sunlight.

It's too cold to set up tables outside, but news of the event spreads quickly through the town, and it's expected to be a busy day. Inside the sanctuary, pews have been moved to a storage building for the day, and tables line the walls. Families are busy laying out their items, and excitement hums in the air.

Pastor Donegal welcomes them, directing Daisy to the tables they'll use. Anika will have a table to herself. Daisy and Allen move to the table next to hers and begin setting up, while Glenn helps stack her wooden trays on the floor behind the table.

"Did you bring the quilt?" Pastor Donegal asks.

"I did, but we left it in the wagon." Anika looks to Glenn, who quickly offers to retrieve it.

"I would like to hang it on the entry wall, coming into the sanctuary, to make sure everyone entering will be able to get a good look at it."

Dr. Parker and his wife, Clara, wave and walk over. Delaney runs to them for hugs. "That's a wonderful idea, Pastor Donegal! I hope it's well received." Anika smiles and glances around the room.

"Anika, do you need any help?" Clara offers.

"Yes, please. Could you help me get my table set up? I've never set up at a bake sale before."

"You'll do fine." Pastor Donegal waves at Glenn and points to the hall to show him where to take the quilt. Anika watches him go, and her eyes catch Martha watching her. Of course, she is wearing the new dress from Mrs. Flannagan's shop, and not a single hair is out of place. Anika quickly turns away and looks for Delaney.

Clara nudges her. "Don't let her bother you. Savannah and I will help run your table. I'll walk Delaney to the children's room where she can play and have a snack."

"Thank you," she smiles softly, watching the excitement on Delaney's face. Savannah walks up and glances at the table.

"I have just the thing to make this table stand out from the rest, besides you, of course," she teases and pulls out a brilliant blue tablecloth.

"Where did you get that!" Anika gasps.

"I can't reveal my secrets, but the white doilies on top will just be beautiful." They begin to set up and place the trays of pastries across the table. "Do you want all of them out?" Savannah asks.

Martha marches over with her mother, and they stand back, watching them set up. Anika ignores her and continues working.

"No, I think I will save the jelly pastries for last. They have to be dusted with the glazing sugar before serving." Savannah turns to glare at Martha, who sniffs and says, "I can't imagine anyone will want to buy from the two of you." Her mother giggles. "If I remember correctly, baking isn't one of your strong suits, Savannah."

Rhemi walks up behind them. "I imagine quite a few will want to taste Anika's wares," he laughs at his crude joke.

Anika's face loses all color, and she stops moving. Leaning forward, she snaps, "That's Mrs. Coltrane."

"That's a vile thing to say!" Savannah snarls. "You're just lucky Glenn didn't hear that."

Rhemi glances around just in time to see Glenn enter the church hall, intercepted multiple times by well-wishers and friendly greetings. "No worries, he's busy."

Glenn walks in, and the moment he sees Anika's stunned, pale expression, his blood starts boiling. He pushes towards her table. Martha watches Glenn moving towards the table and nudges her mother. They intercept

Glenn before he can get there.

"I meant no offense, Mrs. Coltrane. My cousin, Martha, explained your circumstances. I'm sorry to hear of your husband's death. I'd be honored to show you a happier side of our town after the sale, of course. How would you like to ride in my carriage?" Rhemi replies and moves closer to the table.

Anika is thankful for the separation between them. "As I've said before, no thank you, Mr. Darlington."

"Perhaps you misunderstood me." He straightens his coat, flicking a piece of invisible lint off. "A ride with me could solidify your place in the community. My family owns the bank in town, and we would be happy to put in a good word for you."

Anika looks at him, hoping to see sincerity in his voice. He smiles at her, but his eyes don't quite meet hers —they are too busy tracing her figure. His idea of a ride and hers are most certainly not the same. "No, thank you."

"That's it?" His smile flickers out, and he glares at her. "No reason why?" Anika glances at Savannah, unsure of how to handle this. "I assure you, Mrs. Coltrane, you have nothing to fear from one ride. Certainly, you've ridden plenty of carriages before," he teases.

Fury lights inside her soul. He is drawing too much attention spending time at her booth, and she doesn't wish to make enemies straight out of the gate, but his disgusting jokes are making it harder by the second.

Savannah waves at her mother behind Rhemi's back and points at Allen, her father, silently signaling for help. Martha laughs loudly from across the room, drawing the attention of the people who are beginning to trickle in. She is draped on Glenn's arm and staring up at him adoringly. Anika shoves away the jealousy, thinking of Delaney, and continues working on the table.

"I'm sure there are plenty of ladies who would be honored to ride with you, Mr. Darlington. I am busy." Anika picks up another pastry, and just before she places it on the tray, Rhemi grabs her hand. It's sweaty, clammy, and he squeezes the bones together, causing her to gasp. Her eyes snap to his, and she hisses out a breath of shock. He leans in, ogling her breasts, and Anika's patience snaps.

Before she can talk herself out of it, she knocks over the jug of water, causing it to cascade over the edge and onto the front of his trousers. He leaps back with a shout of outrage, releasing her hand, and she can't help but laugh.

"I don't owe you or anyone else an explanation," she smirks and glances away. "You need to learn how to treat a woman."

The church falls silent, and no one moves for a moment. Glenn walks away from an outraged Martha, leaving her standing with her mouth agape.

"You'll change your tune, Anika," Rhemi hisses before snapping up a pastry and stomping from the room.

"Don't bet on it," Anika calls after him and rubs her throbbing hand.

Savannah bursts out laughing. "Score one for you, Mrs. Coltrane."

Her parents rush over. "Is everything alright?" Daisy asks.

"Nothing Anika couldn't handle," Savannah says. "Let's help her clean up."

Anika wipes her hand as if she can wash away the feel of his touch. She balls her hands into fists to stop the trembling and begins to wash up the floor.

Allen watches Glenn stalk Rhemi's retreating form and hurries to stop him. "Don't do anything rash, son. All eyes are on you. Don't make it worse for her," he whispers.

Glenn nods and glowers with rage as Rhemi nods at him before leaving the church. "He better run," he hisses under his breath.

"Now isn't the time, son." Allen leads the way back to the table, stopping to visit with friends along the way.

"Are you okay?" Glenn asks, and glances at his sister, Savannah. Before she can speak, Anika cuts her off.

"Yes, of course. Now let's sell some pastries."

Glenn grins down at her, and she ignores him as she moves to greet her first customer.

Anika spends the remainder of the day laughing, selling her delectable pastries, and mingling with the church members. Initially met with some reserve from the women, the atmosphere changes as the pastries begin to find buyers. Glenn stays close to the ladies, ensuring they are treated with respect by the available men. Delaney, too, makes new friends, and the quilt manages to fetch an impressive eighty-five dollars in a raffle.

"Pastor Donegal, you must be thrilled with today's outcome," Daisy exclaims.

"Yes, our town folks really showed up today." He clears his throat, glancing at Glenn before focusing on Anika. "The sale of the quilt was a success, though it came with one stipulation."

The family falls quiet, and Glenn steps behind Anika to listen. "The purchaser asked that the creator of the quilt deliver it."

"That shouldn't be a problem," Anika says, glancing at Delaney, who is happily munching on a cookie and twirling in her dress with a friend.

Glenn stares hard at Pastor Donegal before asking the question they all want answers to. "Who bought it?" Anika adds, sensing his discomfort.

"Rhemi Darlington," he replies.

"That lecher!" Savannah snarls.

"Savannah!" Daisy chides, hushing her.

Anika laughs at the absurdity of the situation. "Eighty-five dollars is a lot of money. The children need it. I can handle one simple drop-off."

"Well, that's not all. He also requires that the creator go for a carriage ride with him before he will pay."

"Over my dead body," Glenn scowls.

"Why is he so obsessed with that stupid carriage?" Savannah whispers.

Anika wraps her arms around herself in a protective gesture Glenn has come to know well. "That is enough," she snaps. "Pastor, can we speak in private, please?"

"Of course." He guides her into his office, and Glenn follows, only to be stopped by Anika.

"You're making a scene, Glenn. Go back to your family!" She hisses, pushing at his chest and trying to close the door.

Just before the door closes, he leans in and whispers, "I'm so proud of you, Anika, and how you stood up for yourself today."

Shock has her stopping in stunned silence. Glenn pushes into the room and closes the door.

"You will not be alone with that pig. I don't care what he paid." Glenn turns to the Pastor. "I will buy the quilt."

Anika glances at the Pastor and blushes in

embarrassment. "You will not. We just have to outthink him, Glenn."

The Pastor grins with delight at this change of direction. "I like the way you think. What do you have in mind, Mrs. Coltrane?"

"What exactly did he say?" she asks.

"He said he wants a ride with the creator of the quilt. Word for word."

Anika grins and smooths her skirt. "Very well then."

"Not happening, Anika," Glenn rumbles. "The church members are already gossiping. It will only get worse if you are alone with him."

Pastor Donegal's eyes narrow. "Is that so?" Glenn nods at him and crosses his arms over his chest.

"It doesn't help when you act like a buffoon," she snipes back at him and turns back to the Pastor. "Besides, I'm not the creator of the quilt. It was made by your mother's sewing group—all nine of them. I merely assembled the final product."

Pastor Donegal bursts out laughing at the shock on Glenn's face. "Perfect. I will take those names from you."

Anika gives the names and turns to Glenn. "You will wait until I leave before following. I won't have them spreading more lies about us." Glenn frowns and watches her leave.

"You have a bit of a problem on your hands, don't ya son?"

He turns back to the Pastor. "What do you mean?"

"You have to choose between holding onto the past or being thankful for what remains. It's time to look forward to all God has in store for you." He walks around his desk and stops in front of Glenn. "When you're ready,

God is waiting to heal you, son."

Glenn drops his head. "I'm trying, but I don't know how to get back, or even if I can."

"Son, you are allowed to be angry, to scream, but you are not allowed to give up. Allow yourself time, and when you are ready, remember, he never left you. He is beside you, patiently waiting."

"Thank you."

Glenn joins his family outside as they ride together to the cemetery. After the wagon is parked, Glenn lifts Anika down.

"We'll only be a moment," Anika says softly. "Delaney?" She opens her arms and lifts her from the wagon.

Hand in hand, they walk across the cemetery. A solitary little team. Them against the world, and shame strikes him hard. "We don't deserve them, do we?" he asks softly.

His parents glance at him in surprise. "What an ignorant thing to say!" His mother hisses at him.

"Mom!" Savannah gasps.

"They need us, just as much as we need them. God is amazing, son. You have your eyes on the mess, instead of the message. Look at them. They are not defeated." Daisy turns to climb from the wagon.

Allen jumps down and lifts her before she can move. He tells his son, "They are victims of tragic circumstances, just like the rest of us, and no one should have to walk through a storm alone."

They walk away, and Glenn smiles through tears at his sister. "Well, hell. I guess they just gave me what for."

"Yes, they did. Now help me down."

Anika watches Delaney lean down and wipe the

dirt off her sister's mound. She takes a flower from her dress that Clara had pinned on earlier in the day and places it on top. Anika doesn't wipe the tears that flow away. There is no shame in mourning a life cut short. Dropping to her knees, she refuses to look at Saul's grave. Delaney wraps her arms around her mother's head and holds her tightly to her small chest. Anika sobs for what is lost and gives thanks for what remains.

"Thank you, Angel. I needed this. You are my greatest treasure, Delaney." Anika sniffs and jerks at a noise behind them. Delaney's eyes fly open wide when she realizes that the Ward family surrounds them.

Allen, Daisy, Savannah, and Glenn all watch quietly.

"Mama, look!" She says with tearful joy. "We have a new family now."

Daisy clutches Allen's arm and turns her face into his arm to hide her tears.

"That's right, you do," Allen declares hoarsely. Glenn is stricken by the child's words as if God shot them straight into his soul. He realizes how selfish he has been. Anika looks at her daughter and smiles.

"God is good, isn't he, Delaney?" Anika whispers.

"Yep. I'm ready to go home now," Delaney says.

"Yes, let's go home." Glenn offers her his hands to help her stand up as Savannah teases Delaney and races her back to the wagon. Allen and Daisy watch as Anika takes his hand, and they smile when Glenn doesn't drop it until they get back to the wagon.

"God is good," Daisy whispers.

Chapter 17

"Watch, Mama!" Delaney calls and waves from the back of a pony.

Anika smiles and waves back, calling out, "That's my girl." Allen is leading her around, for her lesson just as Glenn and a customer exit the barn near them.

"I'm thrilled, Glenn. She will be a fine addition to our stables." Dayton Patrick shakes his hand just as Allen calls out to her.

"Just a few minutes more, Anika, and she is free to go." Allen leads Delaney and the pony back into the barn to start the cool-down process.

"I'll wait here," Anika replies.

"Good morning," Anika smiles at Glenn and his handsome friend. Dark hair, well-dressed, in denims and a wide-brimmed hat, he bows slightly.

"Anika, I'd like you to meet Dayton Patrick. He owns Patrick Plantation in Kentucky."

"Not the Patrick Plantation, home of Survivor?" she gasps. Dayton grins and pushes his hat back on his head.

"You know of Survivor?"

"My Daddy used to say that he was the only horse that could take several thousand people on a ride at the same time, if you were lucky enough to see him race."

Dayton laughs along with Glenn and stares at the young beauty. "Your father sounds like my kind of man," he teases.

"Thank you. He was an avid horseman." Delaney runs up and throws her arm around her mother's waist interrupting them.

"Mama, did you see me? Mr. Allen says I can learn to trot next!"

"I did see you. You're a natural. Delaney, this is Mr. Patrick."

Delaney curtsies, "It's nice to meet you. Mama, can we have lunch now?"

"Of course. Excuse me, gentlemen, it's time for lunch. It was nice to meet you, Mr. Patrick."

"Who is that?" Dayton asks after they walk away.

"Anika Coltrane, widower and my current nanny."

Allen watches from the door of the barn and steps out, "Why don't you stay for lunch, Dayton, and we can go over the final details." Glenn glares at his father when Dayton replies with a laugh. "I'd love to."

Daisy sets an extra place at the table and hurries upstairs to tell Savannah that they have a handsome guest.

"Really, Mother. I'm a little old for you to play matchmaker."

"Old? Please, you're beautiful and smart. Any man would be lucky to marry you. Now change and join us for lunch."

Anika laughs and takes the now sleeping baby from her. "I'll be right down. Don't wait for me," she calls out and hurries to help Delaney get cleaned up. When they enter the dining room after feeding the babies she's surprised to see a seat next to Dayton. He stands up quickly and waits for her to sit down. Delaney glares at him and moves to take a seat next to Savannah, who covers her grin with her hand.

"You didn't have to wait for us," she sits quickly. Glenn offers thanks, and they begin passing the food around.

Dayton holds the bowl of rolls out to Anika, "Where are you from, Mrs. Coltrane?"

She hesitates and glances at Glenn, who avoids her eyes. "Virginia."

"Call me Dayton, please. Virginia? I thought I caught an accent," he teases. "Do you ride?"

"What kind of Virginian would I be if I didn't?" She

laughs.

"My mama is the best, especially when she wears her denims," Delaney declares, causing Anika to blush and the family to laugh.

"Savannah can ride too," Daisy intercedes and nudges her with a foot under the table. Dayton glances at Savannah with a smile.

"Tell us, Dayton, which horse are you looking at buying?" Savannah asks, taking the hint from her mother.

"Starlight has potential, but I'll have to come back in a few months and see how she is growing."

"You're buying my pony?" Delaney asks in a heart-broken voice.

"I-," Dayton hesitates and looks at Anika in surprise.

"Delaney, Starlight isn't yours. She belongs to the Wards," Anika explains. Delaney glances down at her plate and sniffs. Daisy hugs her close and stares at Allen with a glance of concern.

"We breed horses to sell, Delaney. You know we can't keep all of them, sweetie," Glenn tries to explain.

"Yes, Mr. Ward," she replies without looking up.

"Delaney, do you remember the story of Survivor, the pony from Kentucky?" Anika asks.

"Yes, Mama," her eyes light up as she looks at her mother.

"Mr. Patrick owns her, and he's looking for a new horse to train. Is that right?"

"Absolutely, but it takes time to know if a pony is going to show the traits of a racehorse."

Delaney claps her hands together in excitement, "Oh, Starlight is fast, Mr. Patrick."

"Maybe you could show me after lunch, with your mother, of course?"

"Mama?"

"That would be up to Glenn," Anika replies with a smile.

"That sounds fine. I have work on the south fence. Dad can help you." Anika smothers her disappointment and listens as Delaney talks excitedly about the horses.

"Sounds like you have a budding racer on your hands, Mrs. Coltrane," Dayton says.

"I'm afraid you may be right," Anika replies with a laugh.

"It would be a good idea for you to see Starlight stretch her legs, Dayton. Why don't we all go?" Allen suggests.

Glenn clears his plate and carries it to the kitchen, leaving the family to finish up.

Savannah watches her brother leave with a frown and looks at Anika, who is watching Glenn's retreating back. Anika covers the disappointment quickly and returns to the conversation as Savannah watches and wonders if all men are stupid or is it just her brother?

"Lead the way, Miss Delaney," Dayton teases after lunch is over.

"Delaney runs almost as fast as Starlight does," Allen teases.

"Savannah, are you coming?" Anika pleads silently with her eyes.

"Of course, I wouldn't miss Delaney showing off."

Dayton walks ahead, opening the door for the ladies and joins Allen on the walk to the barn. Anika turns twice to look for Glenn, only to have to hide her disappointment. Savannah nudges her, and she realizes Dayton was speaking to her.

"Have you been away from Virginia long? What is your family name?" Dayton asks as he slows down to walk beside her.

Anika wraps her arms around her midriff and looks at him. "I have. My father was Thomas Bowden."

"Thomas Bowden, the attorney general for Virginia?" Dayton asks, stunned by the new revelation.

"You knew him?" Anika eyes him in shock.

"Of course. I had the pleasure of meeting him in Washington." He also remembers a mention of his death in the newspaper. "I'm so sorry for your loss." His voice holds true compassion, and Savannah wraps an arm around her shoulder in comfort.

"Thank you. We have good friends here now, but I do miss home."

"Perhaps you could visit sometime for a race, I mean all of you, of course," Dayton quickly corrects himself.

"Oh, I don't know," Anika starts to say but Savannah interrupts her.

"I don't know if you know it or not, Dayton, but our winters are intense. It makes travel almost impossible."

"Of course, the races are not until spring," he responds, looking to Anika to answer.

"I should go check on Delaney," Anika starts to say, but once again, Savannah interrupts.

"I will go help her saddle up," Savannah turns and leaves without waiting for a response. Anika almost snaps at her but holds her tongue.

"Forgive me if I'm being too forward, Anika. I understand if you aren't interested in seeing a race." Dayton looks away, disappointed but understanding that it is an awkward position to be in. What doesn't make sense to him is why the Attorney General's daughter is having to work as a nanny to survive.

"How did the daughter of the Attorney General end up as a nanny? Didn't he leave you an inheritance?"

Anika stares at him in shock. "That's none of your business, Dayton."

"I'm sorry, I spoke too quickly. I was surprised, forgive me."

Anika stares at him and avoids his hand when he reaches for her. He's handsome, kind, well-off, possibly attracted to her. It is only fair that she be honest with him. "Of course, Dayton. It's a long story and to be honest, we were not speaking when they passed."

"I see. I hope you don't hold my big mouth against me and will consider coming to Virginia."

"To be completely honest with you, Dayton, I'm in no position for a suitor as I'm under contract for two years for this family. If they choose to come see a race, I would love to visit."

Dayton smiles, revealing a dimple in one cheek, and she

is surprised to find that she likes him. "I guess I will just have to work extra hard to make sure you all come visit in the spring. Until then, could I write to you."

"Why?" Anika asks.

Dayton laughs, "I like you. I see a beautiful, mature woman, with similar interests, and I'd like to get to know you better. Is that so wrong?"

Anika blushes and looks at him, "Dayton, surely you have a string of young women beating down your door. I... I'm not looking for another husband."

"What about a friend?" He asks, turning his hat in his hand. Her relief is instant, and her smile quickly follows.

"A friend would be nice."

The rest of the afternoon passes in excitement. Dayton is thrilled with the way Starlight performs and leaves promising to return in a few months to see how she's progressing. Anika waves as he rides off and turns to Savannah with narrowed eyes.

"What was that, Savannah?" she snaps.

Savannah shrugs her shoulders, "Dayton only had eyes for you, besides he's handsome, rich, and very kind. You could do worse."

Anika stomps up the porch steps. "I'm in no position to leave the boys, Savannah."

"True, but a real man would be willing to wait."

"It's not him, Savannah," Anika whispers, stopping in the hallway upstairs.

Savannah sighs and hugs her. "I know, but a girl can never have too many friends. Besides, a spring race would be fun to go to."

"That's true."

"We would need new dresses for the races. Mrs. Flanagan will be thrilled," Anika teases.

"True, that's always a good thing."

"Until spring, then," Savannah teases.

Glenn works until the sun sets on the fence. His feelings for Anika grow stronger with each passing day.

He's just not sure what to do about it. She deserves someone clean, and his soul is tainted with the blood of the dead. They haunt him day and night. If only the nightmares would let up.

When he returns to the barn, he joins some of the farmhands in a drink. Whiskey is passed around, and they laugh, smoke, and drink until they run out. Then someone brings out a bottle of moonshine. It is well past two a.m. when he returns to the house. He stumbles upstairs, heading for his room, when Anika hears him. She steps out of the boys' room, and Glenn stares at her in wonder. She's a vision in a blue satin wrapper, and his mouth goes dry.

"Oh, I just put the boys down," she whispers and tries to step around him, but Glenn blocks her path.

"Did you wear that for Dayton?" he slurs.

"That's a disgusting thing to say." Anika glares at him, only to smell the sickening scent of whiskey on his breath. "You're drunk, Glenn, go to bed." She tries to step around him, only to hiss in shock when his arm shoots up, blocking her path.

"I'm sorry, that was mean." Glenn lifts a hand and trails his finger through her hair, which is tumbling down her shoulders.

"Yes, it was," she says breathlessly. Once again, she tries to step around him, but Glenn isn't ready to let her go just yet.

"Are you my new nightmare?" He leans down, brushing her hair away from her shoulder and inhales her scent, trailing his hot mouth over her collarbone. The combination of his whiskers and mouth has chills erupting all over her body.

"Glenn?" she gasps and backs up into the hallway

wall.

"I've dreamed of you, Anika. Touching you, kissing you," he nips at her shoulder causing her to gasp, and she stifles a moan when she feels the sting of his teeth, followed by moist hot heat. Glenn sucks her throat marking her, and Anika's knees go weak with pleasure.

"Dreamed of loving you," his tongue trails up her neck to her earlobe, "making you mine," he sucks her lobe into his hot mouth, and she fists a hand in his hair, jerking his head back.

"Glenn," she hisses, but passion and whiskey cloud his mind. "You don't know what you're saying," she starts to say, but he claims her mouth, pushing her back against the wall.

'Oh, God,' she thinks because her mind is just as clouded as his. He savages her mouth, sucking, tasting, savoring her, and she gives as well as she takes. His hand goes to the belt of her wrapper, and he starts to fumble with it. Glenn groans and goes still before his full weight slumps against her, shoving her back against the wall. He groans again and falls to his knees.

Anika watches in horror as he passes out and slumps over against the wall. She pushes him over to his side and checks to make sure he's breathing. He's way too large for her to move on her own.

She straightens her gown and rushes down the hall to Savannah's room and knocks. "Savanah, I need some help please." Anika hears her jump out of bed and the sound of footsteps.

"What's wrong?" Her red hair is a mess, and she is holding her housecoat in front of her.

"It's Glenn," she points down the hall and Savannah almost shouts when she sees him on the floor.

"What happened?" Savannah demands as she jerks on her wrapper and rushes with Anika to his side.

"He's drunk, and I can't move him on my own." Savannah's shock is quickly followed by fury.

"Leave him," she turns to leave but Anika stops her.

"Please, Delaney can't see this again," her voice breaks causing Savannah to stop.

"I'm sorry, I didn't think. Try to wake him, I'll be right back," she rushes away as Anika turns to close the bedroom door, so Delaney doesn't hear them.

She returns to his side and bends down, brushing the hair away from his forehead.

"Glenn, wake up." He mutters under his breath and swats at her hand. Savannah returns with a glass of water from her room. "I can't wake him."

"Move out of the way," Savannah orders and waits for her to stand back before tossing the full glass in his face.

Glenn doesn't move except to wipe a hand over his face. "Need some help, ladies?" A deep voice asks from behind them.

"Dad," Savannah slaps a hand over her mouth. "We were trying not to wake you," Savannah exclaims.

"I see that," he walks over to look down at Glenn and snaps, "this is getting ridiculous." He kicks his foot and gets no response. "That's moonshine for you, he will be in a bad way tomorrow. No one is to baby him." He glares at both of them until they agree.

"What do we do now?" Anika asks.

"You both go back to bed. I'll take care of this."

Anika wonders back to her room, slowly, and glances back as Allen drags Glenn to his room.

She can't blame Glenn this time. The truth is that

she wants him, and the desire is only growing stronger. "What am I going to do?" Her savings has grown, but she doesn't have enough to buy her own place, and the boys are not old enough to be weaned. Delaney will not be raised with another man who drinks.

"Tomorrow, I will have to start looking for a replacement and find a new job," she mutters bitterly.

Chapter 18

Glenn prays for death a few hours later, while his body rids itself of the toxic after affects.

Anika hears him suffering and even angry with him, her heart can't help but wish she could ease his misery. Bouncing Quinton on her shoulder, she listens as he coughs and gets sick through the wall of the nursery. When she steps toward the door, Savannah snaps at her, "Don't even think about it."

"I just want to take him some water," Anika bites back at her.

"He has water; besides I don't think he'd want you to see him like this." Savannah looks at her and whispers, "I'm going to take Delaney to visit Clara in town, she has been collecting sewing squares from everyone in town and passing out flyers regarding the Quilting Bee next week. Dad is going with me, but Mom is staying with you. Don't baby him, Anika. This has to stop."

"I know."

Just before she reaches the door she turns back to Anika, "You may want to wear your hair down for a little while. You have a mark," she points to her collar bone.

Anika blushes and her hand flies up to cover it.

"Do you need to talk about anything else?"

Savannah asks gently.

"No, I, uh, we..." she glances at Savannah who starts laughing.

"That's what I thought. Don't judge him to harshly, Anika. Give him a chance to prove he's a good man. I imagine he'll be mortified when he remembers all of this."

"If he remembers it," she murmurs. Memories flash, of Saul stumbling, hands fumbling, followed by pain. Anika takes a shaky breath and wipes at her eyes.

"He can be better than this, Give him a chance. We'll be back."

She doesn't respond as Savannah leaves.

Anika lays Quinton down and pats him while Allen coos at her. "Who's a good baby, yes you are."

Daisy walks in and smiles down at the boys. "They're growing so quickly. I can't believe they three months old. If only we could freeze time and keep them safe."

Anika hugs her, knowing she is speaking of Glenn. "I know it doesn't seem like it, but Glenn will get through this. He has an amazing family."

"How did you survive it, Anika. So much loss?"

"I had no one to fall back on and that would leave Delaney alone in this world. I turned to my Heavenly Father to guide me and Glenn has you. This family is his safe place, he'll come around soon enough."

"I pray you're right. In the meantime, we should start planning the food for the Quilting Bee. Its only two days from now and we're going to have a big turnout."

"I can't wait to see the children's faces when they realize that people do care. The community cares."

Chapter 19

"Mama, why are we sewing bees?" Delaney asks, while helping stack squares of material that Mrs. Flanagan had sent over earlier in the week. Daisy laughs and hugs her close while Anika stops and stares at them with a smile.

"No, sweetie, it's just an expression. We are going to work like bees in a group to accomplish one goal," Anika explains.

"Exactly, and when the sun sets, we're going to have a party, with music, food, and dancing!" Savannah sings.

"I love parties!" Delaney spins in a circle before stopping. "Will we have cake?"

"Of course, and I made your favorite, apple cake," Anika teases.

"I can't wait for the party, but I don't like to sew." Delaney frowns at the stacks of material piled on two tables in the barn.

Savannah picks her up. "We shall suffer through it together, dearest, then we shall party until the sun rises!" The women laugh at Savannah's dramatic tone, and Delaney squeals with laughter.

A dog runs through the barn, crashing into one of the tables as he chases the cat.

"Allen Wade!" Daisy yells for her husband and sets off after the animals while Anika and Savannah rush to straighten the table.

"I'll help," Delaney chases after them, leaving the barn almost ready.

"How many quilts do you think we can get done?" Savannah asks Anika.

"I'm not sure. Each one is two by four feet long. It will go much quicker with so many hands. I'm hoping for quite a good turnout, but I don't know how many will show up."

"I think you will be surprised. They're all curious about you, and any reason to get together and share food usually brings a crowd."

"That reminds me, I've got to get the apple cider off the fire so it can start cooling. I've never made such a huge batch before." Anika rushes out of the main bay of the barn and into a small galley kitchen in the back. It's a simple mudroom-slash-kitchen for the workers. A black cast-iron stove sits in the corner with a cabinet beside it. Over the cabinet are a set of wooden shelves, with spices on them. The massive black pot is at a rapid boil, and the kitchen smells of fall with cinnamon, nutmeg, and ginger all boiling with apple slices and peels. She hurries to stir it.

"Mmm, smells like heaven in here," Glenn says from behind her.

Anika's heart leaps at the sound of his voice. She managed to avoid him for a few days, attempting to let her anger cool. When she struggles to move the pot, he quickly offers to help and grabs it for her.

"Let me." Glenn slides the pot to the countertop where it can cool. The oven will remain warm to help heat the barn.

"Thank you," she murmurs. "It will have to cool for

a few hours, but it should be ready just in time for the festivities. Excuse me." Anika avoids looking at him and tries to step around him, but he stops her with a hand to her arm.

"You and I need to talk soon," Glenn says softly. "I don't remember much of the other night, and what I do remember is a blur. If I did anything that made you feel threatened, I would never forgive myself."

"No, of course not," Anika pulls away from his touch and puts distance between them. She blushes and wishes it were that easy for her to forget. "Think nothing of it."

"I would feel better if you were angry, not this distant, cold disappointment I get every time you look at me." Glenn runs a hand through his hair and steps toward her, causing her to back away.

Anger rushes through her, hard and fast, until she is trembling with the need to lash out at him. "God, that it was as easy for me," she hisses and stomps toward him, flushed with fury and shoves him back away from her. "If I could, I would box your ears! Now is not the time for this discussion."

Shocked, he stares at her, and guilt rides him hard. "Then when? You have avoided me for two days."

"Glenn, it isn't my safety I worry about, but my daughter. If Delaney had seen you like that," her voice goes hoarse and falls silent. She straightens her shoulders and meets his eyes. "I promised myself she would never be in that situation again, and you made me break that promise." Fury has her blushing. "I will do the job you hired me to do, but I can't... just leave me be." She storms from the kitchen, bumping Savannah on the way out, almost causing her to drop the linens she has brought.

"Forgive me," she calls as she passes her. Savannah sighs and watches her go before turning to him.

"You need to give her some space. After the way you treated her, I'm surprised she's still here," Savannah says and places the cloth down on the counter next to the pot. Picking up the large spoon, she mixes the apple cider while she waits for her words to sink in.

"The way I treated her?" Glenn tries desperately to recall the events, but the combination of moonshine and whiskey has left his memory hazy.

Savannah taps the pot and carefully places the spoon down on a plate before turning to face him. "When she came to my door, she looked a little... flustered, Glenn. Red, swollen lips, messed-up hair, and a bruise on her neck."

"No," horror fills Glenn's eyes as he steps to the door, observing Anika laughing at something Delaney says. "I wasn't myself. Surely she would have said something if I..." He drops his head and turns back to his sister.

"Glenn, what's happening to you?"

"It's the nightmares." Glenn scrubs a hand over his face. "I don't sleep, and whiskey helps. They used to be of the war, now they are of Sue." Haunted eyes meet Savannah's, and she almost weeps for the pain she sees.

"I drank too much, and you know the rest."

"I see. After the bake sale, you were supposed to come to the homestead. Perhaps tomorrow we could try again."

"That's it? No yelling or berating me?" Glenn questions, surprised by the lack of reprimand.

Savannah pauses, her expression thoughtful. "You're doing enough of that for both of us. You need to apologize to Anika." She turns towards the door and stops. "I'd do it soon. Dayton made it clear he was interested in her, and I found her writing a letter today, and she was crying. I'd wager she's planning on leaving us."

Glenn's heart almost stops at the thought of her departure. "That's not gonna happen."

"No. You're doing enough of that for the both of us. You need to apologize to Anika." She turns and stops at the door, "I'd do it soon. Dayton made it clear he was interested in her, and I found her writing a letter today, and she was crying. I'd wager she's planning on leaving us." Glenn's heart almost stops as his eyes harden at the thought of her leaving. "That's not gonna happen."

Anika watches Glenn leave and returns to the house to change into a new violet dress with dark purple trim and a high collar. "Let's have fun today, okay, Delaney."

"Yes, Mama. Can I go play now?"

"Of course," she laughs and gives thanks for the quick healing she sees in her daughter.

As she brushes her hair, she leaves the sides up and the back down, pulling a few curls to the front to cover her neck. Her heart pounds, and her body reacts when she thinks of his hands and mouth on her. It is clear to her that he has no memory of the other night, and thankfully, she doesn't have to talk about it with him.

Nervous energy has her chewing her bottom lip. Dayton made it obvious he was interested in her. Anika never dreamed she would consider marrying a stranger, but he seems kind and was amazing with Delaney. Her heart calls her a liar, and her body agrees.

"I am thinking only of Delaney and our future." She

opens the drawer by her bed and finds the unsent letter. It is for an advertisement for a wet nurse. With the wages they are offering, it will not be hard to find a new post. Picking it up, her hands tremble. A dog barks excitedly, causing her to jump and drop it back in the drawer. Wagons pull in with women and men loaded, children laughing and waving, and excitement builds. Today will be about making happy memories, she promises herself as she heads outside.

Chapter 20

Dr. Parker and his wife Clara arrive with Mrs. Flanagan and several other women from the church, followed by multiple wagons. Each woman brings food, and soon the barn is buzzing with laughter. The men head to meet the new pony, Starlight, and tend to the horses. Glenn promises to return for food around lunchtime.

Martha Darlington arrives in Rhemi's prize carriage with her mother, bearing special mason jars tied with festive ribbons. "Mrs. Ward, I hope you don't mind, but Mother and I brought these just for this occasion. To celebrate our first annual Quilting Bee for the Orphanage. I thought we could share some of that famous cider and toast to new beginnings."

Daisy smiles, "That's so thoughtful of you. Is Rhemi coming?"

"He couldn't make it, unfortunately. He was called out of town on business. But he left us in charge of the carriage."

"That's nice of him. Please come inside. I'll just take those to the kitchen."

"Nonsense, you stay and welcome your guests. Two more wagons have just arrived. Point me in the direction

I need to go." Daisy smiles and instructs her where the galley kitchen is and hurries to welcome the new arrivals. Anika watches from her seat. Already, the women have begun assembling the quilts, and with so many talented quilters, they will have amazing results. Each seating section is set up in stations: one for sewing squares together, another for batting, whether newspapers or old clothes, and the last for sewing the pieces together.

Daisy quickly motions for Savannah and Anika to join her in greeting the families and welcoming their guests. Delaney plays with new friends and chases the dogs, causing everyone to laugh. Mrs. Henriette brings the twins to Anika with Savannah's help, and the women gather to play with them. They are passed around until Quinton decides he's had enough. His cry calls to Anika, and she hands Allen over to his grandmother, and he quickly settles against her throat and hides his face in her hair.

"I don't know how you're managing two of them at the same time. I'm worn out with just the one," Natalie, a young mother, says.

"They are good, as long as their bellies are full," she smiles when his hand pulls a fistful of her hair.

"Just like any man," Mrs. Flanagan calls out with a laugh.

"I should help Mrs. Henrietta get them to sleep, excuse me."

Anika returns forty-five minutes later and joins Clara at the sewing table. The women laugh and welcome her back.

"I'd forgotten how it feels to be part of a community," Anika murmurs as she listens to the women laughing, teasing, and talking about their lives.

Martha watches with narrowed eyes as Anika laughs and greets people like a lady of the manor. Gritting her teeth, she slips away into the kitchen. "Shoo, filthy beast," Martha kicks at the cat, who continues to ignore her and clean its paw. With a glance around the galley kitchen in the barn, Martha rushes to the counter where the large pot of apple cider is cooling.

"Yes," she uncorks a bottle with a pop and prepares to drop two caps full into the pot, as the nasty old man had instructed earlier.

'This is potent, only a few capfuls for an entire pot. Do you ken what I'm saying? The longer it sits the stronger it will become, and this has been sitting for two weeks.' Old man Sutton grins at her and spits his chew into a pot while Martha struggles not to gag.

'Yes, I understand, now give it to me.' She presses the coins into his hand, surprised when he grasps her hand tightly.

'Listen closely, girlie, this shine is potent, like poison if used in the wrong way?' Martha jerks her hand away in revulsion and snaps at him.

'I won't, and you speak of this to no one or my Father will be persuaded not to look the other way regarding your... establishment."

Moonshine is a serious business. The liquor business is full of bootleggers and criminals, just the sort she shouldn't have dealings with. His eyes darken, and he grins, revealing his blackened and missing teeth. 'You shouldn't threaten a man's livelihood, Miss Martha.'

'True, and you shouldn't threaten a woman in love.' She tosses him another coin and grabs an extra bottle to hide in Anika's room. Dark, greedy eyes stare at the coin and at her as she storms back to her fancy carriage and wonders what

poor sob got stuck with her. He follows and steps out onto his porch in the mountains and glares at the young man who helps her back into the carriage.

'Get me out of here, Rhemi.'

'My pleasure, cousin.' He gives a quick salute and jumps inside the carriage.

'Did you get it?' he asks staring at the bottle in her hand.

'Of course," she laughs, 'now we will both get what we want. Glenn will never look at her the same way again.'

'I will be glad to look at her,' she will pay for embarrassing him. 'I will get my carriage ride, one way or another. It took days to get the smell of old ladies out of it. I'm only sorry I have to leave on business, but she should be good and desperate when I return.'

The cat rubs against Martha's leg, jerking her from her reverie and reminding her why she's here. Quickly, she pours splashes of pure moonshine into one of her special jars, followed by cider. "One extra splash, for good luck." When this hits her, they will never trust Anika again, she thinks with a grin. She covers the jar with a cloth and sets it up on the top shelf, pushing it back so no one will see it. "I'll give this one to her myself."

Voices and boots are her only warning. Martha shoves the cork on haphazardly to the bottle of shine before shoving it on the wooden shelf above the pot and hurries out of the kitchen, just missing Spot, the family dog.

Spot runs into the kitchen with a large bark, causing the cat to screech and leap away. She jumps onto the wooden shelves above the pot and knocks the bottle over, pouring the full contents of the bottle into the cooling liquid below. Spot grabs the cork and runs from the room, chewing on his prize as the cat leaps down.

Two hours into sewing, Daisy signals it's time for a break and drinks. "Ladies, I shall return with cider, but this year's brew is made by Ms. Coltrane, and if you're nice enough, she may give you the recipe." The ladies laugh.

Martha jumps up, "Let me help." Anika watches with a frown but is distracted with Delaney as she asks if they can go play at the house.

Martha is quick to make it to the kitchen before Daisy and begins to ladle cider into each jar, being sure to place Anika's at the back of the serving tray. "My goodness, Martha, you're fast. Thank you for your help."

"Of course, Daisy. I'm not much of a seamstress, but I'm glad to help in any way I can. You fill them up, and I'll start serving." Martha leaves and begins handing out cup after cup to the twenty women, young and old. Some refuse the brew, but Martha is insistent that this is for the community. "Just one drink in honor of this day. Lest we forget how fortunate we've been and just how important this task that Ms. Coltrane has given us."

Once Daisy finishes handing out the glasses, Martha sighs with relief. "Proverbs 19:17 says, 'Whoever is generous to the poor lends to the Lord, and he will repay him for his deed,'" Clara says. 'Father in heaven, we ask that you bless this day so that we may do your work. Amen."

"Amen," the women chorus.

"Cheers," Martha says, encouraging everyone to drink. All the women are soon sipping away and munching happily. Lunch is served, and Anika is aware the moment Glenn enters. Flushed from the heat, she happily fills plates for the men who move down the line and smiles at Glenn as she hands one to him.

"Are you having a good time, Ms. Coltrane?" He asks as she hands him a plate and sips on her second cup of cider.

"Oh, my yes."

Glenn can't help but notice the blush on her cheeks and the way she smiles at him has his mouth watering, though, not for the food. "You're holding up the line, Son." Allen teases and nudges him. The plates are filled with fried chicken, biscuits, and pickled beans.

Martha glares from her seat and makes her decision. Perhaps it wasn't enough? She slips back into the kitchen, finding to her surprise the bottle is no longer where she left it. The old bootlegger obviously didn't know what he was talking about. Even if it is found, no one will know it was hers. "If three pours did nothing but make her giggle, then let's see her handle a full bottle." She pulls the bottle from her bodice, removing the cork, only to jump at Savannah's voice outside, coming closer. Panicked, she dumps the whole bottle into the pot. She quickly shoves the cork on and stashes it back in her bodice.

"Are you lost, Martha? Or just looking for some unsuspecting man to ensnare?"

Martha laughs and grabs a spoon to stir, just as Savannah walks up behind her. "Daisy asked me to grab a tray of cookies. Men have large appetites, at least your old fiancé did if I remember correctly." She pushes past Savannah with a laugh and carries the cookies straight to Glenn standing next to Anika's chair.

"I heard you liked sweets, Mr. Ward, perhaps you'd like to try one of these?" Her dress is cut to draw attention to her body. Any other man would have jumped at the opportunity.

Glenn looks at her and wonders at her audacity. For one so beautiful, she comes off as desperate. His stomach drops at her insinuation. He steps back and tips his hat. "No, thank you. We are just returning to work on the fence, and my appetite is quenched." He turns and marches outside.

"I bet it is," Martha hisses glaring at Anika before she stomps to the table and slams the tray down.

Anika watches Glenn leave, barely aware of Martha. She shakes her head feeling slightly dizzy. "I think I need to eat something," Anika grabs a plate and loads it with food and quickly finds a chair near the door. "So hot," she murmurs as she nibbles on a piece of chicken.

Martha watches and panic is beginning to set in. This was only supposed to get Anika drunk, not all the women from the church!

Her mother walks over to Martha and whispers, "Do something!"

"We need to go now. I did something stupid," Martha hisses and whispers in her ear explaining about the bottle.

"They all think they are better than us. What will happen when he returns, and you are the only sober one left," her mother cackles.

Martha's eyes fly open wide, "Mother, you're a genius!"

"Of course. I think it is too cold, and they need to drink?" She suggests.

Martha smiles and turns on her heel to follow one of the stable hands outside. "Excuse me, you look like just the sort of man I need. I mean with all your muscles," her hand covers her mouth in a pretend blush, "It's just that the women are cold, and we were wondering if you could add more logs to the stove."

"Of course," he slides his sweat-stained hat back and grins at her. "Anything for such a pretty lady."

Martha giggles and hurries back inside, to wait. "It will take about an hour for it to warm up in here, keep filling their cups, mother."

"Do we have a count on the number of quilts?" Savannah asks Daisy.

"I'll ask Anika." Daisy looks around and finds her attempting to sew a panel.

"Blast it!" Anika hisses as she misses and pokes herself again.

"Perhaps you should take a break, Anika." Mrs. Flanagan says with a laugh.

"Would you mind getting a count of the finished quilt, Anika?" Daisy asks.

Anika sighs and wipes at her brow before standing up. Swaying on her feet she grabs onto Daisy. "Is the floor moving?" All sound ceases as the blood rushes to her ears. Three women jump up to help.

Martha hurries to help, "Here drink this. It's hot in here." Pressing a cup of cider into her hand.

One woman fans her as Anika sips at the drink. "Perhaps I should've eaten my lunch. Thank you, ladies, I'll be fine."

Daisy returns with a plate of food. "Here, eat something. Clara and I will count."

"You remind me of my Mother. I miss her," she smiles at Daisy. "Glenn is lucky to have you."

"Thank you, sweetheart, now eat," she laughs and points at the plate.

"Yes, Ma'am." The food fills her belly, but she still feels strange. Soon the barn is warm enough to dry meat, and Martha makes the rounds with multiple glasses of cider on a tray.

"My, but it's hot in here," Clara mumbles and tugs at the collar of her dress a half hour later.

"I thought it was me," Anika says as Martha offers a fourth glass of cider. "I really shouldn't, but it is so hot."

"I could open a door, if you wish?" Martha offers while she refills glasses.

"Martha, you're so right, we should open the doors," Clara declares with a giggle as she fans herself.

Daisy burps, and all the women laugh in shock, "Oh, my goodness."

"I'm dizzy," another woman murmurs, and Martha's smile widens as she eyes her mother.

"I want to dance," a young girl declares and jumps up to find her friend.

"We need music," another shouts.

"Let's sing." Three of the youngest start to sing.

"I can play the fiddle," Anika murmurs, and soon someone is pressing one into her hands.

Clara laughs and spins on the floor, pulling Daisy and some of the older women with them. Delighted, Martha laughs as she watches the scene unfold.

"What's that noise?" Allen says puffing on his pipe.

"Sounds like... music?" Dr. Parker states.

"More like someone killing an instrument," Glenn mutters and they start walking towards the barn. The closer they get, the louder it is, and they begin to move faster. They open the doors to the barn and all the men stand, staring, with their mouths open in stunned, fascination. Heat rolls out in waves and flushed women, giggling, laughing, spinning, and swaying all move like a wave towards them.

"What the--?" Dr. Parker watches Clara with a grin of surprise. "Josiah! I've been waiting for you." She grabs him and whispers in his ear as she pulls him to the floor.

"Clara Parker!" He shouts in laughter at her lewd suggestion.

Martha frowns as she watches from the corner. Allen laughs as Daisy picks up a harmonica and tries to play. Glenn covers his mouth with a grin when he realizes the noise was Anika trying to play to the fiddle.

"Why won't it work?" Anika mumbles and tries again, sawing at the strings.

Martha tries to intercept him as he makes his way to Anika, but she is stopped by two girls dragging her to the floor to dance. "Let go of me, you fools!" Martha hisses but they just laugh and imitate her.

"Let go of me you fools," one of them slurs.

Anika saws at the strings, stopping to frown. "I think it's broken."

"It works better when you hold it the right way," Glenn flips the violin over and hands it back to her.

"I knew that" she frowns at him.

"Looks like they started without us," one man says.

"Can't have that," another laughs and rushes to get his instruments. One has a banjo, another a harmonica and Anika has the fiddle.

The moment they start playing Anika smiles, "Oh, I remember." She jumps up, swaying on her feet and waits for the room to stop spinning before moving towards the men. Anika doesn't wait for a break in the music, she jumps in. Everyone stops moving and then a roar of approval sounds out from the men.

Glenn watches in awe as she plays and holds her own with the men.

"Glenn! I've been waiting for you," Martha rushes up at him and smiles, "Can you believe this behavior? It was Anika," she starts to say but he turns away.

Glenn barely takes his eyes off Anika and smiles when she hands the fiddle to another man and takes a break.

"Excuse me," Glenn murmurs, completely ignoring Martha, and follows Anika.

"Anika?" he calls out.

She spins with a grin and snaps, "Where have you been? I want to dance."

"Well, lead the way, my lady," Glenn says pulling her into his arms.

"I love to dance," Anika says spinning in his arms and he laughs. "Glenn, I think the floor is moving," she says happily leaning against him.

"What have you been drinking?" he laughs.

"Only Apple Cider, it's my special recipe."

"I bet it is." Glancing around Glenn can't help but stare at the sight before him.

Anika stops and frowns up at him, "Glenn?"

"Yes, love?"

"You have way too many clothes on. It's hot."

Glenn throws his head back and roars with laughter. "It's not funny, I can't breathe." She pulls at his shirt to untuck it and he grabs her hands.

"Okay, honey, I think we should take a walk and cool you off."

"I want to touch your skin, taste it," Anika stops moving and looks at him in wonder and leans over to whisper, "I dream about you sometimes too."

His mouth falls open again and he's forced once again to grab her hands. "Anika," he groans and glances to his right, where movement catches his attention. Martha is holding a small bottle in her hand and she tosses it on the floor, smashing it to bits before dragging her mother to the exit.

"What was that about?" Allen calls out as he rushes to get a broom to sweep up the shattered pieces, frowning when he recognizes the color of the glass.

Glenn frowns when Anika pulls away to stare at the crowd of people. "So hot," she murmurs.

"Look how long my arms are?" One excited voice calls out. She waves her arms around and laughs hysterically, while her friend laments, "Mine are tiny," and falls to her knees sobbing.

One of the older women begins to stomp and clap her hands on the dance floor to a song that isn't playing.

Allen finishes cleaning up, and Dr. Parker frowns at his wife. "Clara, what have you been drinking?"

"Only apple cider," she says swaying in his arms.

"I'm hot, I think I'll have another," Daisy slurs.

Savannah laughs at the crying girl on the floor and pulls her up to dance, while Clara gasps and turns on Daisy.

"Mrs. Ward, I do believe you are drunk."

"Don't be ridiculous, I'm a grandmother," she slurs and leans her forehead on her husband's chest. Allen glances down at his wife and looks around the room.

"Hot, dizzy," over and over the same complaints begin to filter through, Glenn frowns and pushes the hair back on Anika's shoulder.

"Anika, tell me what you put in the cider."

Joy explodes on her face. "Magic, Glenn." She throws her arms in the air and points at the ceiling, "I wished for you and here you are!"

Glenn can't help but laugh at her. Anika stops moving and looks at the doors. "I'm so hot."

"Just what on earth is in that cider?" Dr. Parker snaps distracting Glenn.

Angry voices erupt as the men begin to gather their families and attempt to load them in wagons.

"But I want to stay, and dance," another woman shouts.

"I want more magic cider," another one cries, and Glenn is struck by a horrible thought.

"Martha!" he hisses.

Dr. Parker grabs Clara's hand and marches her to a chair. "Stay here," he orders. "Show me this cider," he demands. Clara frowns at him.

"That was rude," Clara murmurs and sniffs, trying not to cry. Anika takes her hand and squeezes gently. Her head is pounding and her heart beats in time to the rhythm in her head.

Allen guides Daisy to a chair next to Clara. "Daisy isn't feeling well, could you look after her for a minute, Clara?"

"Of course, Allen."

"Stay with them, Anika," Glenn orders.

Anika sticks her tongue out at Glenn's retreating back and the women all laugh hysterically.

Glenn ignores the laughter behind him and hurries to the kitchen followed by both men. They are surprised to find a half empty pot. Dr. Parker pours a cup into a mason jar and holds it up to the lantern. "It looks the right color," he sniffs and frowns. "I don't smell anything." Allen is about to taste it when a cat jumps down from a chair.

"Meow," the cat rubs Glenn's legs. He ignores her for

a second until he hears the sound of glass on a wooden floor. A small brown bottle spins, as the cat smacks it with her paw.

His stomach drops when he picks it up and finds it empty.

"Old man Sutton," he hisses. A well-known moonshiner, Glenn glances at the bottle and the pot.

"If she put the whole bottle in the pot, we're in for a long night," Allen says with a laugh.

"No, she had two bottles, Dad." He glances at the pot and they all fall quiet for a moment.

"Give me some good news, Doc," Glenn murmurs.

"The good news is that they didn't drink the whole pot, the bad news is, well, you know how a hangover feels."

Anika watches Glenn walkaway with a frown and stands up slowly, to keep the room from tilting. "He's always leaving," she murmurs, wiping the sweat from her brow.

"We used to swim when we got hot, Allen and I." Daisy pats Clara's hand and points to the door. "The pond stays cold and it's so romantic, night swimming."

"I can't swim," Clara says with a glance at Anika.

"I love to swim," Anika grins and picks up her skirt. "Where is the pond, Daisy."

"You head across the main field, towards two large pines. If you ride straight at them you will come to some trees, just keep going and you can't miss it."

"Don't tell Glenn, he's very bossy, with this do this and do that, nonsense," Anika slurs as Daisy explains how to get to the pond a second time. Giving a wave she stumbles through the mass of people and goes outside. Instantly, the cold air rushes over her and she inhales.

"Thank goodness. It's so hot..." she mutters as she walks to the barn and finds a mare tied to a post. "Hello, beauty, I will call you Miss. Jerry." After a few attempts she is able to climb into the saddle.

"Go, Miss Jerry," she exclaimed, giving a swift kick. The horse trots away, bouncing Anika along. The first pieces of clothing to come off are her shoes, followed by her purple jacket. "That is much better," she sings, dropping more pieces of her clothing as she goes.

Allen and Glenn are distracted by angry voices and hurry to help the guests leave. "I'm sorry about this, Sheriff," Allen apologizes to him as he has too each of the men who are loading their wives into wagons.

"This was one interesting afternoon, Mr. Ward," Sheriff Austin says with a laugh. "Not everyone will think it's funny, you best be prepared for some questions on Sunday."

"I'd like to come by your office on Monday to discuss this," Glenn hands him the bottle and tells him about the other smashed one.

"I'll ride over tomorrow and have a chat with Old man Sutton. For now, I'm gonna enjoy seeing my wife like this," he laughs as she giggles, and the children tease her.

Allen nods and tips his hat as the last of the guests leave. Thankfully Mrs. Henrietta agreed to stay over for the night and help with Anika and the twins.

Daisy and Clara are giggling and munching on cookies in the main house when the men return to get them.

Glenn glances around and frowns. "Where's Anika?"

Clara giggles and covers her mouth. Daisy pushes her softly and straightens to her full height. "Cookie?" She holds up a tray.

"Mother," he starts to snap but Allen stops him with a hand to his arm.

"Daisy?" Allen frowns, "Where is Anika?"

"I want to go to bed now, Allen," Daisy says smiling up at her husband.

"Me too," Clara says.

"You didn't answer the question, Mother," Glenn yells.

Daisy leaps to her feet and shouts back, "Don't raise your voice at me!"

"Mom?" Glenn stares at her in shock.

"Anika could be in danger, where is she?" Allen asks sweetly.

"We promised we wouldn't tell Glenn she went swimming in the pond." Clara smooths her skirt and pulls at Josiah's hand. "Now, can we go home," she whispers.

"Swimming in the dark!" Glenn shouts.

"Don't be such a prude son, your Dad and I swim naked," Allen smacks a hand over her mouth with a shout of laughter.

"This isn't funny," Glenn hisses.

"She couldn't have gotten far on foot, son," Allen says. "Take blankets."

Clara pushes a hand to her head. "Josiah, my head hurts," she whispers.

"Time to go home," Dr. Parker says firmly.

Glenn runs from the house to hear, "Where's my dang horse?"

His stomach drops when he sees a lady's shoe. "Problem, Fred."

"My horse is gone. She must have loosened the

reins." He scratches his head while Glenn runs into the barn. He returns leading an old mare.

"Here Fred, use this one. I'll bring your horse back when we find her."

The seconds tick by like minutes, while he waits for Fred to leave. The moment he mounts, Glenn runs into the barn and mounts his stallion.

Panic is beginning to set in as the sun begins to set deeper in the sky. He quickly rolls up a blanket and ties it to his saddle before leaping on his horse. He thunders towards the fields stopping when he comes across the first piece of clothing and a second shoe.

His mouth goes dry when he finds her waste jacket. A few feet later he finds a large purple skirt. Jumping from the horse he picks it up and looks around. "Anika!" he shouts, no answer.

"Dang," he climbs back on his horse and rides fast.

Anika urges the small mare on, stopping to remove her clothes as her body seems to be burning up. Wearing only a camisole, she hums softly and struggles back onto the mare, before giving a swift kick of her heels. "Swimming, swimming, I love to swimmm," she sings loudly and giggles.

"Over the hill and through the trees," she reminds herself and claps her hands with glee when she sees the trees. "It's so dark, Ms. Jerry, how will we find the pond?"

The mare snorts and keeps walking. "Of course, my apologies, you know where we're going." When the pony stops a few minutes later, Anika gasps and slides from her back and pats her. "You're the best Ms. Jerry I know. Thank you."

The pond glistens, reflecting the sinking son in the sky above. It's a clear evening and Anika stares at the pond and sighs. "So beautiful," her breath puffs out a misty warning of the temperature dropping, but she is oblivious.

Anika dips a toe in the pond and grins before walking straight into the water. She swims, rolling over and floats.

Glenn thunders through the trees, startling Ms. Jerry and causing her to stomp her feet and run away. His breath rushes out when he sees Anika floating in the pond. "Thank God," he mumbles and leaps down. He ties his reins to a tree branch and jerks a blanket from the back of the panting horse.

Anika ducks her head in the water and pushes her hair back on her head.

"Anika, come out of the water," Glenn calls. Anika frowns at him and shakes her head no.

"No thank you," she says and swims away from him to the center of the pond.

"Anika you'll catch a cold. It's freezing now, stop playing and swim to me."

"I don't think so, Mr. Ward," and she rolls over on her back and stares up at the stars. "It's beautiful," she murmurs.

Glenn's mouth falls open as he realizes all she is wearing is a thin camisole. He whirls around and wipes a hand over his eyes and starts praying. "Lord, I'm gonna need your help with this one."

"Come swim with me Glenn," she calls softly, teasing him and his heartbeat pounds in his ears.

"Anika, stop playing and let's go home," he calls to her again.

"It's like I'm floating in the stars Glenn."

"The stars aren't out yet, Anika," he informs her.

"Kill joy," she snaps and giggles.

It takes all his strength to not turn and watch her in all her glory. Desperation has him throwing out the first thing that comes to mind.

"Delaney is waiting for you. Don't you want to say good night to her."

"Delaney?" Splashing as she rolls over the water spins around her and she frantically turns looking for her daughter.

"Oh, no! I've lost her! Delaney!" She screams and dives under to look for her. Quickly realizing his mistake, Glenn whirls around and finds to his horror that she is gone.

"Anika!" he runs straight at the water, diving in to find her.

The water is deep, black, and impossible to see in. Which way is up? Delaney! She screams in her mind. Something grabs her arm and jerks her. Anika starts fighting as she comes face to face with her dead husband.

Saul grins, with skin hanging from his face, rotting teeth, a missing eye and he laughs at her, pinning both arms to her side he drags her body against his. Anika fights, choking on pond water and struggles to break free.

Glenn drags her from the water, screaming, and coughing. He's forced to pin her arms down to stop her from hurting him. "Anika," he shouts, "look at me."

"Delaney!" she coughs out, "Please let me get Delaney."

"She's at home, Delaney's at home." Anika stops struggling and stares up at him.

"No, Saul took her," she cries and starts struggling again. Glenn puts his face beside her ear and talks softly, holding her tight to his body.

"No, Saul is dead. He'll never hurt you again. Delaney is at home, let's go home."

"Home?"

Glenn presses a kiss to her forehead. "Home," she sighs and her teeth chatter. "Glenn, why am I so cold?"

He laughs softly and releases her arms. Glenn rests his forehead on hers, "Because you decided to go swimming." Anika wraps her arms around his neck, holding him in place.

"Your wet," she murmurs as she kisses his mouth softly, "and you taste good, feel good."

"So do you," Glenn groans and grabs her arms, unwrapping them from his neck. "I have a blanket," he climbs up from her, ignoring her protests, and hurries to his horse.

When he turns around he finds her walking towards him and his mouth falls open. He should turn around but part of him wants to burn this image in his mind's eye. To say she is beautiful is an injustice to the word. "Anika, you're killing me."

"I'm cold, don't you want to warm me up?" He takes two steps towards her before he makes himself stop.

"I'd love to, come here," he demands.

Anika smiles and rushes into his open arms. Glenn wraps her in a blanket and pulls her against his chest.

"Let's get you dressed and home."

Anika pushes back and starts to unbutton his shirt. "Not yet," she grumbles.

Glenn laughs and grabs her hands. "Anika, we have to go."

"Don't you want me, Glenn?" she says pressing her breast into his chest.

"More than the air I breathe, but not like this." He

steps back drawing the blanket tighter around her and turns to his horse, grabbing her clothes.

"He didn't want me either," she says swaying on her feet. "Saul said no man would ever want me again."

Glenn's head drops, "He was a fool and you deserve better." Anika pulls on her skirt and jacket, she doesn't bother with her stockings. "I don't feel well, Glenn." She runs to the bushes and vomits. Glenn is beside her to help keep her from falling over and after they are home he stays with her when she weeps through the vomiting and pain, he promises to make sure Martha doesn't hurt her again.

"Is Mama going to be okay?" Delaney asks from the doorway. Glenn tucks the covers around Anika and puts a basin near his bed.

"Come here, sugar." Delaney runs to him oblivious of her tears she buries her face in his neck and sobs.

"Please don't let my Mama die."

Glenn holds her close and his heart swells with joy at the trust she is showing him. "I promise, Delaney. Everyone gets sick sometimes. No one will ever hurt her again."

"Okay, Mr. Glenn, but why is Mama in your bed?" she sniffs.

"Well, I thought it would be the best place for me to take care of her. How about I get you tucked into bed and read you a story. If we leave the door open I can hear her."

"Do I get to pick it?" she teases.

Glenn chuckles, "Of course. You get into your night gown, while I finish up and I will be right there." He sets her on her feet, smiling as she pads from the room.

Delaney stops and watches how tenderly he cares for her mother as he dips a clean cloth into fresh water and wrings it out before washing Anika's face. She groans and clutches at her head, rolling away from him.

"Mr. Glenn, can we pray for Mama?" Delaney asks before she leaves.

"Of course. Come here." He reaches for her hand and rejoices in his heart when she grips it. His voice is hoarse as he starts to pray, but it grows stronger with each word.

"Heavenly Father, we pray that you will lay your healing hands on those who are sick. Have compassion on all who are suffering, so they may be delivered from these dreadful circumstances."

"In Jesus name, Amen."

Delaney sighs, "Amen."

Chapter 21

Old man Sutton hears the warning whistle from his sons and steps from the barn with his shotgun. He walks swiftly towards the stump in front of the house and leans his gun up against the porch before picking up his axe to chop wood. Eli, his oldest son helps him gather the split pieces and stack it.

A bird call sings across the morning air, informing him of the number of men coming. 'Three'

Their horses round the last bend in the roughhewn road giving them a view of the cabin overlooking the valley below. "Good morning, Mr. Smith," Sheriff Austin calls, keeping a close eye out for trouble.

Scrubbing a hand over his beard, Sutton glares at them and sinks his axe into the stump. "What can I do you for?"

Eli grins and reaches for the axe only to stop and glare when Glenn's hands go to his rifle. Behind him the second brother raises up his gun. "You don't need to do that, son."

Old Man Sutton stares at Glenn and then smiles broadly. "Allen, good to see you. How's Mrs. Daisy doing? Can I offer you some coffee?

"Just fine and as beautiful as ever, I'd love some

coffee, thanks" Allen steps from his horse and pumps his hand, laughing.

"Forgive my son, he still has to learn to not judge so quickly."

"They always thinkin, they know more'n us, don't, they?" He turns to Glenn, "Son, I was sorry to hear bout your wife, I hope your sons are well?"

Glenn stares at him and looks back to his father in confusion before answering, "Thank you sir. My boys are getting fatter every day."

"That's good, come inside." He grabs his rifle and hobbles up the small porch going inside.

"Eli, I hope your family is well?" Allen says following closely behind.

"Yes, sir. Thanks to your generosity."

"None of that now, I think we both know that we helped each other." Allen turns to Glenn, "You missed a lot when you were away."

"I can see that." He murmurs as he follows them inside the modest two room cabin. Sheriff Austin sips on his coffee and leans back before pulling the bottle from his pocket.

"What can you tell me about this bottle?"

Eli glances at his father and John hisses out in frustration. "Knew she was trouble, in her fancy carriage and all. I told her to only use two splashes per batch. Why? What'd she do with it?"

Glenn sighs and runs a hand over his face. "She used two full bottles."

"What?" Eli shouts while his father stops puffing on his pipe and leans forward.

"Was anyone hurt?"

"Depends on the definition," Glenn snaps.

"Don't be thickheaded, son. We believe she poured one full bottle into the apple cider at the Quilting Bee. Not sure about the second bottle, she crushed it on the floor of my barn."

John sits back in shock as Allen explains in more detail.

"Daisy was sick for twelve hours straight as well as Savannah. Ms. Coltrane has been sick for two days."

"Two days? Tell me her symptoms," he demands.

"Hot, fevered, chills, hallucinations, tightness of breath, and vomiting. Not to mention headaches," Glenn answers hoarsely.

Eli goes to the cupboard and pulls down a small brown bottle. "This is lemon and honey. Mix it with a cup of boiled water and serve it like tea. It will help with worst of it. Remember, lots of fluids for her," he instructs offering the bottle to Glenn. "Two teaspoons per cup."

"Thank you."

"Why would that girl do this? I warned her that it would be dangerous?" John turns to the Sheriff. "What are you gonna do about this?"

"Not much I can do. Martha swears that Anika did it and that you are lying for her," Sheriff Austin replies with a sigh.

"That girl ain't right in the head, talking about true love..." John Sutton turns to look at Glenn. "You? Was she was talking about you?"

"I never gave her reason to believe anything of the sort," Glenn hisses and stands up to move to the window.

"You best beware of her, scorned women are dangerous," Eli says.

"I can see that," Glenn sighs. "She made all the women in my family sick."

"It's worse than that, son. It could have poisoned them all."

Allen covers his face with his hand when he thinks about his wife and daughter. "What are we gonna do about this?" he asks Glenn.

"Thank you for your time, Mr. Sutton. I will see what I can do, but right now it's your word against hers."

"I'm sorry Allen that you and yours were hurt. If there's anything I can do, let me know," John offers.

"I will. Thank you."

As they ride away from the small house, Glenn looks at his father, "You have some explaining to do."

Allen waits until they are halfway down the mountain to pull on his reins. Sheriff Austin slows his mount, "I'll be asking around town and visiting Martha again. Don't do anything rash."

Allen doesn't promise, instead he watches the Sheriff ride away before speaking. "John Sutton and his sons helped us when the raiders came and tried to burn down our home and barn. In return I provided them with fruits and vegetables for their families. It seemed like a fair trade."

"I wish I'd known that" Glenn says staring back up the mountain.

"You didn't ask." Allen rides away leaving his son in silence.

"Guess he's right, I do have a lot to learn."

Chapter 22

Sunlight streams through the dress shop's windows highlighting the delicate lace and intricate patterns of the bonnets and dresses around them. The air carries the scent of freshly crafted fabrics, and the rustle of silk and cotton adds a subtle melody to their conversation.

"Stop fretting, Martha, you'll only give yourself worry lines. They can't prove that you put a few splashes into her cup or the pot. I can guarantee that the church members will be in an uproar over this incident. In fact," she says toying with the new bonnet in Mrs. Flannagan's dress shop, "with the right nudging I can promise the will run that girl out of town on the next train."

Martha grins, "Mother, I love your devious mind. Did you see how they were acting," she cackles loudly. She dabs at her eyes and sniffs struggling to get herself under control. "It was more like a half a bottle in her cup, and that's before the whole bottle I poured in the pot," she says cackling even louder.

Martha, her laughter echoing through the shop, holds up a necklace to inspect it closely. The sunlight glints off the intricate design, revealing the fine craftsmanship of the jeweler. The delicate sparkle dances in the air as Martha admires the piece, her mind consumed with the satisfaction of their mischievous plot.

"I heard she was sick for four days" her mother insists.

"Not nearly sick enough," Martha snickers. "One shouldn't be surprised that someone of his lineage doesn't know quality."

Mrs. Austin moves quietly through the aisle behind them and must fight with her anger. She was sick for half a day on just three glasses of that cider, what that poor girl must have gone through! She hurries away from them and goes in search of her husband.

Sheriff Austin marches into the main office of the First National Bank and smiles as he's greeted by a clerk. It is a small building in the center of town and quite busy this time of morning.

"I need to see Mr. Darlington, Jess."

"Jessica," she smiles. "I hate that nickname and you know it, cousin."

"I do know it."

Jessica's eyes flick around the room and she scurried around the desk. "I can't let you see him right now, Sheriff. He's with some important visitors."

"I'm afraid this isn't a social call, Jess. I need to see him now."

"Give me a minute." She hurries to the office in the back and knocks on the door.

A few moments later she is followed out by a flustered looking man. He is dressed in his best suit and his smile doesn't quite reach his eyes when he greets him. "Sheriff, what can I do for you?"

"Mr. Darlington, I think you will want to hear what I have to say in a more private setting."

"I see, follow me." Thomas Darlington is used to being in charge. This is an awkward position for him to be in and having the Sheriff show up at lunch time, his busiest time of day is not good for business. He leads him to a small office in the back of the building.

It has two chairs and a small table. "We need to keep this short Sheriff. I'm meeting with investors and I don't want to keep them waiting."

"Let them wait." Sheriff Austin watches the color drain from Thomas's face as he is told of the incident at the Quilting Bee.

Standing up, Thomas paces and rubs a clean cloth over his face to mop the sweat that has suddenly appeared. "That is a shame to hear, but I can assure you my wife and daughter would never do such thing."

"I have witnesses-"

"Old man Sutton is a known moonshiner, Sheriff. No one would believe his word over ours and without evidence Sheriff, I'm afraid your hands are tied."

"Thomas, I don't need to tell you that if the citizens of our town can't trust you, they won't trust their money with you. Why I'd even go so far as to suggest that the investors you are talking to might catch wind of this incident and cause problems for you."

Thomas loses all color in his face and plops into one of the chairs. "Sheriff these investors are here to invest in a new textile mill. There's even talk of building a new bank. I don't need to tell you what that would do for our town. The jobs it will bring to the families and money to this community are desperately needed for recovery after the war."

"I know that, Thomas, but this tantrum could have killed someone. It's out of my hands. Nineteen members from our church, all women were affected, including my wife!" He snarls, "You need to get a handle on your wife and daughter!"

"Perhaps an extended visit out of town? I must go to Boston to meet with an architect to discuss plans for the new bank. I will take them both to Edith's sister. Would that work?"

"I think that's a good idea, but you must explain the next time they pull something like this, I will arrest them both. That will mean newspaper articles, Thomas."

"I understand, Sheriff. Thank you for your discretion. They will be on the first train for Boston in the morning.

Chapter 23

Anika sits in the chair near the window and nurses Quinton for the first time in three days. "Hi sweet boy, I've missed you." He grins behind her breast and she sighs in contentment as Savannah returns with another pot of lemon tea.

"Oh, not again. No more lemon and honey. Tell your brother, I'm much better. It's been four days," Anika hisses in exasperation.

"I'm not telling him that," Savannah laughs. "He's been really worried about you. He slept in the chair beside you for two days, Anika."

"Don't say that out loud. He shouldn't have done that," she clears her throat reaching for the tea and sips on it while the baby plays with her hair.

"I'm sorry to say it, but Dad had his hands full with mom and so did Mrs. Henrietta. Delaney wouldn't leave you, only if Glenn promised he'd stay with you."

"I'm so sorry, Savannah. I'm just mortified," Anika whispers looking down at Quinton who smiles at her.

"Sheriff Austin is downstairs. He wants to speak to you about the incident."

"I'm sure he does. Tell him I'll be down when I'm finished with the twins." Quinton fusses when she moves to burp him. "I know big boy. You both need to make up for lost time."

"Mom's feeding the Sheriff her apple pie. He said to tell you to take your time. Should I go get Dad and Glenn to be with you while you talk to the sheriff?" She asks cautiously.

"No. I've caused enough trouble for now. Let's see what he has to say first."

"Okay." Savannah hurries from the room looking worried.

Forty minutes later Anika walks into the main room and stops in shock when she finds the entire family present. Daisy, Allen, Glenn, and Savannah are all waiting for her.

"I'm sorry to keep you waiting, Sheriff." Butterflies erupt in her stomach and she clasps her hands together in front of her trim waist.

"No problem. I'm tempted to send you away, so I could have a second slice of Daisy's pie." Everyone laughs as Anika walks slowly in and sits in the only space available, next to Glenn. He settles back, draping an arm over the seat behind her.

"First, let me say that it's nice to see you have recovered. I'm not sure what you were told, but I have some new information for you all." He clears his throat nervously, not sure how they are going to take it.

"Can you tell me what you remember?"

Anika glances at Glenn, bunching her hands tightly in her lap. "I'm so sorry, my cider made everyone sick. I have no idea what went wrong, Sheriff. I swear it's the same recipe as any other cider."

Glenn sits up and takes her hand, "You did nothing wrong, Anika."

"He's right. Martha confessed to pouring a bottle

of liquid into the batch of Apple Cider." Sheriff Austin, continues, "We know she bought it, but she is not owning up to that. She says it was on the shelf in the barn when she left."

"That's outrageous!" Daisy shouts.

"I found her in the kitchen stirring the cider, I just thought she was trying to make up for being a jerk," Savannah exclaims.

Allen draws Daisy close to his side, "What else?" he demands.

"Mrs. Flannagan heard her talking about pouring half the bottle into Anika's cup."

"Half a bottle!" Glenn leaps to his feet and begins pacing. "That explains why you were so sick, Anika."

"I'm confused. Could someone please explain to me what was in the bottle?" Anika asks.

"Aged moonshine. It's stronger than most anything you could get in any saloon. In fact, the longer it sits, the stronger it becomes." Sheriff Austin explains.

"Why would someone need something that strong?" Daisy demands.

"It can be useful for surgery," Savannah answers hoarsely. "Wounded soldiers, sometimes screaming from pain, need something to make it manageable, but it's a last resort."

The room falls quiet as everyone stares at her.

"I see." Anika stands up and walks away from them towards the window to stare outside. "It's shocking to think someone could hate me so much that they would go to such extremes."

"Sheriff, something has to be done!" Allen demands leaping to his feet. "She could have killed someone I love. My wife, my daughter, my grandsons..." his voice fades away as he looks at his family.

"I understand, Allen. My wife was sick for half a day. I can't imagine what you went through, Mrs. Coltrane, unfortunately it's your word against hers."

"How are we supposed to protect our family from this?" Daisy asks softly.

"You can't. I'm the problem, Daisy. You don't know the vile things she said to me in the dress shop." Anika shutters.

"What did she say?" Daisy asks, but Anika shakes her head no and turns away from them.

"Anika, it could help explain why she did something like this," Sheriff Austin says.

Trembling, Anika turns back to look at Glenn. "She said she waited two years for Sue to die and that I would be sorry if I got in the way."

"Why didn't you say anything?" Glenn demands.

"What good would it do? I told her that I was below your class, Glenn. I tried to reassure her that I was not a threat." Anika paces as she thinks.

Sheriff Austin stands up, "I've had a discussion with her father. Martha and her Mother are taking an extended visit to an Aunt in Boston. She won't bother you again."

"Thank you, Sheriff. I suppose that will have to be enough." Daisy says.

"Let me walk you out Sheriff," Allen says.

Daisy leans forward and pours them tea, "Are you alright, Anika."

"Thank you for being here," she murmurs not quite answering the question.

"Of course. You aren't alone anymore," Savannah says hugging her quickly.

"You'd do well to remember that in the future." Glenn says. The clear reprimand in his voice hurts and she walks over to the window to watch Delaney playing with the dogs.

"I can't quite wrap my mind around this. That someone I don't know could hate me enough to harm me." Delaney turns and waves at her and Anika lifts a trembling hand to wave back. I've seen what happens to orphans, I want more for my daughter."

Glenn holds up a hand to stop his mother and sister from speaking. He walks to her near the window and takes her hand. "I promise you that Delaney will never be an orphan. If anything were to happen to you, we will raise her as a member of our family."

"Glenn!" Anika whispers through tears, "You shouldn't make such promises."

"You heard him," Daisy snaps, "You are part of our family now Anika and that includes Delaney."

Savannah grins, "I'm going to take Delaney to see the new kittens. Mother?"

"I'd love to see them." They leave them alone for a few minutes, giving Anika time to compose herself.

"They are not very subtle, are they?" He asks with a grin.

Anika laughs and wipes at her eyes. "Not really."

"I'm glad to see you feeling better." Glenn stares at her until she pulls her hand away from his.

"Thank you, for everything. Delaney tells me you prayed for me."

Glenn nods and sits down to pour himself some tea, "I haven't prayed in a really long time."

"If my illness brought you closer to the Lord, then I am thankful for it. I wish I could remember more, but it's all a blur."

"What do you remember?" he asks sipping the steaming liquid.

"Flashes really. Dancing, music, laughter, and... water. Sinking, drowning, and Saul." Anika shutters and stares at him.

Glenn grins, "Nothing else?"

"No." Her eyes narrow suspiciously, "Why?"

"Just curious," he smiles behind his cup.

"I don't like that smirk, Glenn Ward. Tell me what I did?" She demands with a hand on her hip.

"I didn't know you could play the fiddle?"

"Oh," memories flash of cheering, dancing, and playing. Anika drops her face into her hands. "Lord, save me," she whispers and Glenn laughs out loud.

"How will I ever show my face in town again, let alone church!" She says sitting next to him.

"Don't worry about it." Glenn pulls her hands away. "I will have a talk with the Pastor and he will explain everything on Sunday to the congregation."

"Thank you." She pulls away and grabs her cup. "There is something good that came out of this. I doubt I will be asked to plan the Fall Carnival."

They laugh for a few minutes and Anika leans closer to him. Her smile fades and she touched his arm. "I would like to say, that this has been eye opening for me in some ways. What I do remember, is a feeling of happiness, no, that's not right, just a release of the pressure of everything. I understand now why Saul drank so much and you..."

"Don't compare me to him," Glenn snaps, interrupting her. "I am not a drunk who beats women."

Anika stares at him in shock, "I never said that."

"You thought it, though. I need you to understand that some men can handle drinking better than others. I would never hurt you."

"Can you truly say that, though?" she asked softly. "I don't remember half of what went on the other night." Flashes of his hands and mouth on her remind her why she should be careful.

Glenn falls silent, "I can only beg your forgiveness, Anika. This has been eye opening for all of us. Will you forgive me?"

"Yes, of course," she murmurs, avoiding his eyes.

He turns her face back to his with a finger to her chin. "Look at me," Anika looks up.

"Please say you will stay. I understand if you want to leave, but I don't want to lose you."

Anika is quiet for a moment and struggles with the urge to run, but her heart isn't in it. "I'll stay."

Glenn releases a breath he was holding and grins. "Excellent."

Anika smiles. "Now let's just hope the church members are so forgiving."

"We will face them together, next Sunday."

Chapter 24

"How quickly a week passes," Anika murmurs as they walk into the church. It doesn't escape their notice how quiet the inside of the sanctuary is, though it's packed with parishioners.

Whispers, nudges, judgmental glances and no one moves to greet the family.

Daisy clutches onto Allen's arm as they take their seat in the back of the church. Anika and Glenn carry the boys, while Delaney runs off to Sunday school.

"Welcome." Pastor Donegal smiles and glances around the church. "The first order of business this morning is to discuss the incident at the Wards home last week.

Glenn starts to rise, only to stop when the Pastor lifts his hand.

"Mr. Darlington is here and has a few words to say."

Clearly flustered the banker hurries to stand in front of the pulpit. Only Rhemi is sitting next to him this morning. As he kept his promise and sent the women away.

"I'd like to first offer my sincere apologies for the accident that occurred. My wife and daughter are away helping take care of an ailing family member, but let me assure you, they are sorry for the misunderstanding.

Grumbles ripple through the church and Anika stops Glenn from speaking with a hand to his arm. Anger rips through his body when he thinks of how sick she was.

"I can assure you that nothing like this will ever happen again. My wife felt terrible that this hurt the children, and as a token of our good will, we have ordered blankets for the Orphanage for every child, along with winter coats for each one."

Excitement rushes through and everyone begins smiling and talking. "That's wonderful. Now let's put this incident behind us and move forward as a church family," the pastor implores.

After a lesson on forgiveness, Anika hands the baby to Savannah and walks outside to find Delaney.

"Mama!" she waves excitedly and starts to make her way towards her Mother.

Anika gasps when a man steps in front of her. Her stomach drops, "Good morning, I'm trying to get to my daughter," she says softly and tries to step around him only to be blocked.

"No problem, Ms. Coltrane. I just want to make it clear that when the Ward family is through with you, I would be glad to hire you for your... services." He glances down at her dress and tips his hat before stepping around her, hurrying to his wife.

Tremors shake her body as she lets it sink in. "Mama! Come watch me skip," Delaney shouts, knocking her from her shock.

"Coming, Delaney," she plants a fake smile on her face as reality strikes home. Some dreams are meant to stay dreams.

Rhemi straightens his tie as he climbs into his carriage and watches Anika with growing anger and resentment. It's time to pay her a visit and claim his ride.

Chapter 25

Savannah is working inside the homestead cabin when she hears a horse outside. Stepping out into the cool air she watches her brother nervously. "You're off early."

"I am." Glenn slides down and ropes the horse to the front porch. "I meant to come with you on Sunday night, but it was a crazy day. So, here I am." He dusts his jeans and stomps his way up to the porch. He glances around and then back at his sister who has gone oddly silent. She is wringing her hands with apprehension.

"What's got you in such a state." The house looks well cared for. It is a small one-bedroom cabin, built by his grandparents.

"Glenn, I'm not sure I'm ready for you to see this." She holds up a hand to block him, but he laughs.

"Your starting to worry me, Savannah. What on earth have you two been up to? Brewing anything illegal?"

"Wait!" She tries to say, but he jumps around her and throws open the door.

Kerosene lanterns glow along the walls, casting a golden light around the room. Memories flood in and he smiles. "It looks good. You guys have been busy. It's so clean." He frowns when he realizes there is no furniture save a tall table.

Savannah follows wondering how he is going to react. "Anika helped me get it clean. She hasn't been back since I... decorated," she laughs nervously.

Glenn walks forward to the table and looks down. Six by eight-inch images of soldiers, both confederate and union line the table all surrounding a larger tin type. It is a thirteen by ten-inch tintype of a battlefield. The images hanging on the walls at varying heights are all framed in gilded frames, but this image needed no dressing. It revealed the horror of what was left behind. Bodies littering battlefields. Hands reaching up from a silent graveyard, begging for release.

Glenn stumbles backward as the smells and sounds of war batter his mind. Savannah watches in horror as he turns and runs outside, slamming the door back as he goes. He falls into the grass and vomits his lunch. "What have you done?" he gasps when he catches his breath.

"I gave a face to the ghosts which haunt you and so many others, Glenn. I gave a voice to the dead who deserve to be mourned."

Glenn staggers to his feet. "No, you just made the nightmare real."

"I didn't think you were ready. You should have listened to me." Angrily she wipes her tears away.

"Ready? No one needs to see the face of death more than once, Savannah."

Savannah laughs a bitter laugh, but she doesn't back away this time. "Someone has too. When you are ready come back and see what is really here, it is the legacy of the lost and they deserve to go home too."

Glenn is stunned silent when she stops inside the house and slams the door without another word. Inside her dark room, a bag sits in the corner reminding her of the promise she made.

"Soon, Oliver. Glenn needs me right now."

Glenn rides back to his house and stomps inside, to find his family at dinner.

"How could you be part of that?" He demands of Anika.

"What are you talking about? Allen asks his son.

"I'm talking about what Savannah has been doing at the Homestead with Anika's help," he accuses. Anika slowly lowers her fork and stares at him.

"Where is Savannah?" Anika asks softly.

"She hasn't come home yet," Daisy replies.

"I see."

"See what? I don't understand how you could be a part of such a travesty." Glenn turns to leave but before he can stomp away, Anika snaps at him.

"You only understand something if it pertains to you. Not everything is about you, Mr. Ward. Your sister is hurting and though, she hasn't yet shared with me why, I know enough to be there for her when she is ready."

No one speaks for a moment as Allen stands up slowly. "If my daughter is hurting then she shouldn't be doing it alone. Daisy?" He reaches for her hand.

He doesn't ask twice. Daisy grabs his hand and jumps up. "You two coming?" Allen tosses over his shoulder as they leave.

Anika tosses her napkin on the table. "I need to see to the children."

"That's it. You don't have anything else to say?" Glenn is beyond angry. The images are still burned in his mind. He scrubs a hand over his eyes in frustration. Anika stares at him and sighs before takes his hand and drawing it away from his face.

"Glenn, whatever it is that upset you, I had no part of. Savannah has become a good friend, and I'm sure she didn't mean to upset you. Give her a chance to explain it to you. She's your sister."

Her touch floods him and she is surprised to feel his hand trembling. "I wouldn't wish this for her or for you," Glenn murmurs. "You should not have to see..."

"You can't control everything Glenn. Even if you could, I'm not sure you should. I'll get my coat and ask the housekeeper to stay with the kids. You can show me what has you so upset."

The Homestead is lit softly with lanterns when the four of them arrive. "Mom maybe you and Anika should wait outside," Glenn suggests one more time.

"Thank you for your concern, Son, but I will be with my daughter."

Allen stomps up the front porch hoping the noise will inform her of their arrival, but she doesn't come out. "I'm not knocking on my own door," Allen grumbles and pushes the door open. They enter single file into the small room.

Anika allows her eyes to adjust, not sure what she is seeing. It's clean as she and Savannah left it, but all the furniture has been removed except for one table. In the center of the room is a table with a lantern glowing. Daisy gasps when she looks at the table and Allen guides her away allowing Anika and Glenn to step forward. A large tin type in in the center of the wooden surface surrounded by smaller images. On the left side of the large picture are Union solders, on the right Confederate. The center image is a bloody, battlefield. Anika gasps as the horror unfolds in her mind.

Allen and Daisy move slowly around the room looking closely at the images on the cabin walls. At first the images are more of the same, soldiers dressed for battle but if you look closer you see more. Nurses tending the wounded, Pastors reading last rights, Women weeping over the covered body of a loved one. Some of the images are of wounded soldiers in camps set up to care for them.

Savannah steps out of the back room, set up as a dark room and stares in stunned silence at her family. "What are you doing here?"

"Did you take these, Savannah Ward?" Allen asks hoarsely.

Daisy sniffs and wipes her tears while she waits for her daughter to answer.

Anika moves slowly through the images and hear heart stutters. "Saul, experienced this?" Glenn stays close to her in case she needs him and glares at his sister.

"I did," she whispers.

"Why?" Daisy asks her daughter.

"Why?" Savannah laughs a harsh emotional laugh. "Because someone needed to."

"No, Savannah, no one needs to see this," Glenn gestures at the images as if disgusted.

"You look brother, and only think of yourself, but look closer." Savannah marches towards the wall and points. "Tens of thousands of soldiers died, maybe more."

"I know that. I lived it!" Glenn roars. "Live it still, every night in my dreams! Not a second goes by that I don't carry this."

"You aren't the only one to lose someone!" Savannah shouts back and doesn't bother to hide her tears.

Anika nods slowly in understanding as Daisy rushes to her and puts an arm around her shoulder. Of course, Anika could kick herself for not seeing it sooner.

"What was his name?" Anika asks softly.

Allen and Daisy listen in shock as she sobs out her answer. "Oliver." Great heaving sobs shake her body and she finally mourns him. "Oliver," she cries and thinks of all he could have been. Glenn marches to the back room and comes back with two chairs for them to sit on.

Daisy sits next to her daughter, Savannah burrows in her neck and cries until she has no tears left. "You never, ...you didn't, ... I, I don't understand." Daisy stammers.

Savannah laughs and accepts the handkerchief from her father. "I know, Mom."

Glenn walks slowly around the room and he takes in the images. Soldiers, young and old, on both sides of the war. All doing their duty, fighting for a cause they believed in. Women, nursing the sick and diseased. The dead being buried and more.

Allen trails around the room and stops in stunned admiration at the new images. "You took these?" he gasps. "All of these?" Daisy steps to his side and they move slowly through the photographs. Images of buildings, farms, barns, and churches all as beaten down as the men. Like the survivors they carry scars as well.

Glenn runs a hand over a large tin type of a shabby looking General Store. Half the room is missing but customers line up to buy what they can. Savannah watches them and hope sparks as they all stare intently at the images.

"The Sisters of Mercy said I could travel with them as long as I didn't let my photography interfere with the duties of nursing and caring for the wounded. He came in on my second day with gunshot wounds to his side and chest. We did what we could to save him, but he faded a little bit each day. Oliver watched me taking photographs of the soldiers returning from the battlefield, but he never spoke, he just watched." Savannah walks over to the images lining the wall.

"I didn't think much of it at first, because some of the soldiers had broken minds." She glances at Glenn. "You understand?"

"Yes," he replied hoarsely. Savannah travels down the wall. "One day I was storing a tin type in my bag and another one fell to the floor. It was of this church," she walks quickly to the wall and points. They all move closer to look. "The bell took a hit and was knocked from the steeple."

"Pulled from the steeple," Glenn corrects her and Savannah nods.

"Before I could move Oliver spoke. 'Show me.' I showed him the picture and he smiled. 'Now that is a picture,' he said." Savannah laughs remembering and runs a finger over the picture. "For two weeks I nursed him." She points to a picture of Oliver, with a bandage around his head, young, and battered on a cot. "I tried to save him," she whispers and turns back to them.

"The images seemed to give him hope, so I showed him the others. Oliver got so excited, then. He made me promise to retrieve his bag from a friend and give my word that I would see it returned to his brother, Eli."

"What was in the bag?" Glenn asks almost afraid of the answer.

"Tin types, hundreds of them. Like the ones on the table, but much more important. It was his dying wish that the dead be remembered. He spoke of his family, his home, his brother and of all the things he wanted to do when the war was over." Savannah's voice breaks.

Daisy takes her arm and guides her back to the chair. "I didn't love him, not like what you and Dad have." Her eyes snap to Glenn and Anika, but she doesn't say the words. "We were friends. He had the same vision I had. The ability to look and see more." Savannah falls quiet, thinking about her friend.

"When the fever set in, the Sisters told me he wouldn't have much time and on his death bed he made me pen a letter to his family and promise to process the images and see them returned to his brother."

"That is a large promise," Allen murmurs.

Savannah lowers her head in shame. "I couldn't do it," she whispers.

"Couldn't do what?" Glenn asks.

Savannah jumps up and begins to pace, tossing her red hair over her shoulder.

"My images are after the war, his are from the battlefield. Moments captured, of soldiers, impacted by bullets and sabers. Diseased, starved, and mass graves. I couldn't close my eyes without seeing it. I only got through half of them." Guilt weighs heavily on her.

Anika stares at the large battlefield and closes her eyes. These are the images Saul couldn't live with.

"It was an unfair promise, Savannah. His family will understand," Daisy explains.

"While I worked I sent letters to the families of those I nursed, telling them of their last moments. I visited the ones I could get to. I sent the letter he asked me too, but I didn't return the bag. I couldn't get through them. I just needed to come home and heal my mind. Being with you all has a way of washing away the horror, if only for a little while," Savannah explains as her mother hugs her close.

"I had no idea..." Anika says as she stares at the gruesome scene. "Saul came home but he wasn't the same. This explains so much," she whispers. "You must finish them. This is important," she says louder.

Glenn walks around a second time and stares at the faces. So many died, and families will never know how. God speaks to his heart saying, 'Trust me.'

"For I know the plans I have for you, declares the Lord. Plans to prosper you, plans to give you hope and a future," Glenn quotes. He walks over to her and stoops down, taking Savannah's hands in his. "You didn't have to carry this burden alone. Forgive me for being so selfish. I will do better, that is a promise. I will help you with this, but this time you won't be alone. Together we will see your promise fulfilled."

Savannah weeps and throws her arms around his neck, "Thank you."

Anika wipes away tears and moves around again to look closer at the images. All the noise fades into the background, so intently is she looking at a bloody battlefield scene that she doesn't hear them talking. When Glenn touches her arm, she jumps.

"Oh, I'm sorry. Are you ready to go?"

"We can wait a minute if you need too," Allen offers.

"I'll bring her with me." Glenn offers.

Savannah nods. "I'm tired. I think I'll ride with Mom and Dad. Lock up for me," she asks.

Anika doesn't speak as they leave, she just returns to the scene and traces her finger over it. "Saul was a farmer. Not a fighter. The boy who went to war never came home. I used to tell myself that it wasn't him, but a *monster* in the form of the man I once loved. It helped to explain the rage. Looking at this, I'm not sure what to think."

"You've seen enough of this, let's go."

"Why? Do you think I'm too fragile to handle the truth?" Fury strikes fast, and she turns on him.

"Of course not, I'm only trying to protect you."

"It's too late for that, Mr. Ward. I can take care of myself."

"I don't know what you want me to say?" Glenn glares at her.

"Let's go." She stomps towards the door only to jump when he shouts at her.

"Anika, what do you want from me?"

Her steps falter and she turns on him with a glare. Stomping over she shoves him in the chest, "I want you to live! Live for those didn't come home, Glenn. Live for those who came home and were never the same." She shoves him again, shocking him with her strength and rage. "Live for those baby boys who need a Father, Not a monster!"

"I'm not Saul," Glenn grabs her hand and pulls her close. "I'm trying," he whispers. "I promise I am."

"I don't understand, Glenn." She cups his face in her hands gently. "What will it take for you to look and see what a miracle you are?" She pulls away from him and steps back. "I'm sorry, I'm angry at Saul for not being strong enough and I'm angry at myself for not being what he needed and I'm mad at you for not realizing that God has never left you. He is waiting for you to come home."

"I am home, Anika."

"No, you are still on the battlefield. It was never your fight, Glenn. You say such beautiful things to your sister, but it applies to you too. Give all your anger, rage and fury to the Lord and lay it down. It's such a heavy burden you're trying to carry, and you don't have too."

"I know what you're saying, but how do I get from here to there? I'm doing the best I can, Anika."

"Saul used to say that at the beginning. I hope you figure it out soon, Glenn" she replies and rushes outside.

Chapter 26

Anika hears the doorbell ring and frowns. Just when she was looking forward to some time alone. Delaney is at the barn with Allen, and Daisy took Savannah to town for shopping. The twins are being cared for by Mrs. Henrietta giving her some time to herself. Glenn insisted she comes three days a week to help.

When she opens the door her stomach drops. "Rhemi Darlington at your service." Tall, dark hair, and well-dressed he would be any woman's idea of a good catch, except he makes Anika's skin crawl.

"Good morning, Mr. Darlington. I'm afraid Glenn is working in the fields pruning, you just missed him."

"Excellent," he sweeps his hat from his head and leans on the door frame. Dressed in a dark blue suit, he's dressed to impress. "I came for you, Anika. You owe me a ride."

Allen is walking Delaney around the corral next to the barn on horseback for her lesson when he notices the carriage in front of the house. He whistles at Glenn who has just returned from the fields. He trots over on his horse.

"Were you expecting company, son?"

"No. Isn't that the Darlington carriage?"

"Looks like it. Let me go with..." Allen sighs when his son kicks his horse into a full run towards the house.

"I didn't give you leave to call me by my first name, Mr. Darlington." Anika snaps at Rhemi. "You will have to come back another time when Glenn is present."

The teasing light in his eyes flickers out replaced by a violence she recognizes. Anika tries to slam the door, but he jams his foot inside. "Come now, Anika," he sneers. "Surely you can at least hear me out or is that too civilized for you." His face is close enough that she can smell a sweet, foul smelling odor that she can't place.

Rhemi shoves the door with his shoulder ripping it free of her hands and it slams into her shoulder, knocking the breath from her. He steps inside and closes the door shut behind him, locking it. Anika spins to run only to yelp in shock when he leaps in front of her.

"What do you want?" Anika looks around desperate for a way to protect herself.

"I have an offer for you. I'm in need of your particular services." He grins and steps towards her. "I've been waiting for a chance to get you alone." Anika turns and runs into the kitchen. She almost makes it to the back door, but Rhemi is faster. He laughs as he grabs her sore arm. Anika grabs the closest thing she can reach, a black cast-iron skillet to fight him off, but he is much stronger than her.

Rhemi jerks it from her hands tossing it across the kitchen with a crash and backhands her across the face. Anika careens into the small wooden table and chairs.

"Anika," he kicks a chair out of the way. "I'm in need of a wet nurse." He grabs the front of her dress and rips at it.

Anika screams and scratches his face with her nails, attempting to break free of him, but nothing affects him.

Rhemi jerks her up by the upper arms, lifting her from the floor, staring down at her chest. "One with full, round, breasts, erect..."

The click of a rifle being cocked has his blood running cold. "You'd better not finish that sentence, Rhemi."

Anika tries to jerk free of his grip, but he squeezes her upper arms, causing her to scream out in pain. Instead of releasing her, he flips her around and shoves a knife under her chin, pulling her back against his body, he starts backing away.

"Glenn you've had your fun, now it's my turn. Anika's coming with me." His eyes are the only indication of his state of mind. Wild fury, and dilated pupils he drags Anika backwards.

"Glenn?" She pleads. Blood trickles down from the corner of her mouth and the room falls silent. His eyes shift to hers taking in the fear as they plead with him silently to save her.

"Shut up!" Rhemi screams.

Glenn sizes up his enemy. The noise fades from the room as he seeks his target and fires. Rhemi screams, dropping the knife as the bullet barely misses his ear and sinks into the plaster wall behind him. Glenn cocks the rifle again.

"The next one will be through your forehead!"

Rhemi shoves her away from him and Anika runs behind Glenn just as Allen and a stable hand burst through the kitchen door with pistols.

"You could've killed me!" Rhemi screeches.

Allen takes one look at Anika and punches Rhemi. No one moves for a second until Anika laughs, startling everyone and then begins to sob in earnest. Glenn hands his father the rifle and doesn't speak. He picks her up and strides from the room, straight up the stairs and into her bedroom.

Alone in her room Glenn sits in her favorite chair as she sobs and waits for her tears to slow. A basin of water is on the table next to the chair and he gently dips a cloth into it and lifts her chin. A bruise is already forming on her cheek and he tenderly wipes at the swollen corner of her mouth, washing the blood off.

"You don't have to-" Glenn silences her with a look and her tears start again. His gentle touch is her undoing. Anika knows she shouldn't be in his arms, or alone with him, but she can't bring herself to let go just yet.

Glenn sighs when she folds back into his arms and rocks her, waiting for the trembling in her body to stop. He savors the feel of her and struggles to calm his own savagely beating heart. When she tries to push away, he holds on, "Not yet," he pleads.

Glenn blows out a shuttered breath and she realizes for the first time that he is trembling too. Anika relaxes and buries her face in his neck. His warmth, surrounds her, his scent fills her, and she finds in that moment, peace for the first time in years.

"I've killed a lot of people Anika during the War, but never once did I do it because I wanted too." Anika leans back and stares at him. He traces her face with a finger and her heart stutters. "I want to now."

"Glenn?" She whispers, and he stands with her, striding to the bed. Her mouth parts in shock when he lets her feet go and she slides down his body to the floor.

The front of her dress is ruined, revealing a purple lace corset and scratches from his nails across the pale skin. Desire strikes fast and hard. He guides her to the edge of the bed and pushes gently encouraging her to sit down.

"You should clean up now. I need to go deal with him."

Anika sits, pale faced and nods as he turns to leave. Just before he gets to the door, she calls out.

"He's not worth it, Glenn. We need you here. Don't kill him." He nods and stomps from her room.

"Don't kill him, don't kill him," Glenn chants as he storms down the stairs. A minute later, Rhemi is tossed into the front yard and it takes his father and two stable hands to pry him off Rhemi's bloody body.

Glenn laughs and shrugs them off. "I didn't kill him."

Later when the Sheriff comes to collect him Glenn leans into the back of the carriage and tells Rhemi, "Don't you ever set foot near me or mine again. The next time you'll leave here in a wooden box."

"She's trash, Wade! When you're through with her I'll be waiting." His father leaps and grabs Glenn pulling him back before he can finish what he started. The Sheriff drives off before he decides to let Glenn shoot him.

"No, she's not trash - she's mine," he growls.

Allen stares at him in stunned silence. Glenn stops fighting his father, shocked by his train of thought. He jerks free and stomps back inside the house.

Glenn is washing the blood off his fists when his father walks in. Allen steps over the broken chair and steps to the kitchen cupboard, pulling down a decanter of whiskey. Two glasses are poured, and he offers one to his son. Glenn tosses the whiskey back and hisses as it burns its way down his throat.

"The Sheriff says he will hold him overnight, but his father will pay to get him out."

Glenn slams the glass on the counter and Allen falls silent. "I should've killed him."

"What's going on with you, son? You aren't a cold-blooded killer-" Allen jumps when Glenn turns and laughs a bitter laugh.

"You can't be serious, Dad." He steps close enough to see the streaks of green in his father's blue eyes. "I've lost count of the lives I've taken, and I didn't *want* to kill any of them." His hands shake as he pours another whiskey. "He was planning on hurting her."

"Don't you dare use me as an excuse," Anika snaps. Both men jump in shock when she stalks to him and jerks the whiskey from his hand and tosses it in the sink. "I won't be the reason you unleash the rage you carry in your soul, Glenn."

"You have no right to-" Glenn snaps only to stammer in shock when she pokes him in his chest.

"No one else has the guts to say it to you." Anika ignores the noise from the entry as Daisy and Savannah return from shopping. 'The bible says in Peter, 5:8; to be alert and sober-minded, Glenn. The Devil prowls around like a roaring lion, seeking someone to devour.' Don't let it be you," she pleads.

"How easy it is for you to say, but have you forgiven Saul yet, Anika? You carry the same fury reflected in me."

Glenn's anger doesn't scare her because it is tempered by his fear for her. He touches her bruised cheek, swollen lip. The tears in her eyes add fuel to his fire and he shouts at her, jerking free of his father's hand on his arm.

"He was going to hurt you!"

"He wouldn't be the first man to hurt me. No, Glenn I haven't forgiven him, yet. He took away my innocence, my trust in humanity, but I want to forgive him. I trust God will show me how. Do you?" Anika turns and walks past the shocked faces and stomps to her room.

Glenn storms outside and finds Delaney cowering under a tree near the back porch. "Delaney?" he calls out. Delaney looks up with a tear stained face and his stomach drops. "Everything is okay, sweetie."

"You yelled at my Mama," she accuses him.

"I did." Glenn sits next to her on the ground. "Sometimes when people care about each other they yell."

Delaney wipes her eyes with the sleeve of her dress and looks up at him. "Mama says love shouldn't hurt, Mr. Glenn. Did you hurt my Mama?"

Shame fills his soul and he drops his head for a moment to regain his composure. "I didn't strike your Mother, Delaney. I would never hit either of you." Delaney stands up and knocks the dirt from her dress. She walks closer to him and taps his shoulder.

Blue eyes meet hazel, "Words hurt too, Mr. Glenn. My Mama has had enough hurt." A single tear slips free and tracks down his cheek.

"I know, Delaney. I'll ask for her forgiveness. Will you forgive me for scaring you?"

She searches his face and finds something that calms her heart. "Yes, Mr. Glenn," she throws both arms around his shoulders and hugs him tight. Glenn sighs and closes his eyes in shame.

"Thank you, Delaney, you are a very special little girl."

"I know," she giggles and runs inside to her mother.

Glenn stands slowly and walks to his horse. Riding out he prays that God will be as forgiving as this child.

Chapter 27

Pastor Donegal is working on a wooden floorboard on the front step of the church when Glenn rides up on his horse.

"Mr. Ward, your just in time to save me from real work," he says with a grin.

"Glad to be of service," Glenn says with a laugh as he dismounts. "Do you have a few minutes to talk?"

"Of course." He drops his hammer and dusts his hands on his denims.

Glenn spins his hat in his hand nervously glancing at the church behind him. "Let's walk to the barn and tie up your mount."

"Thank you." They make their way slowly to the barn and Glenn clears his throat. "I've got a serious problem, Pastor, and I'm hoping you can help me."

"I'll do my best." He shows him where to tie the horse up and waits for Glenn before guiding him from the barn.

"I do some of my best thinking back here. Something about the water soothes my soul. I built this bench just for this purpose."

Glenn sits nervously on a bench next to the small pond behind the barn and starts to talk. "I almost killed

Rhemi Darlington this morning. He attacked Anika in our home."

"Is she alright?"

"Yes, she's stronger than most." His hands ball into fists, "I'm afraid I scared my family."

"What about yourself?" The Pastor asks softly, "Did you scare yourself?"

"Yes," his hoarse voice is low with shame. "I thought I'd left it behind me, all the killing, but it followed me home." He looks out at the water and frowns.

"What followed you home?" he asks.

"The rage, Pastor. It doesn't let me rest. I thought the nightmares were done after the war, but since Sue passed they've gotten worse."

Pastor Donegal stares at him and takes note of his rough condition. Beard, anger, gaunt look, red eyes, trembling hands, and sighs. "I see. Can you tell me about the nightmares?"

Hardened eyes that have seen the unimaginable stare back at him. "I can't speak of the carnage."

"War is a nasty business. Tell me what bothered you most about being a soldier."

"Surviving," Glenn responds instantly. He glances away, ashamed to finally voice it aloud.

Pastor Donegal closes his eyes in a quick prayer, asking God to guide his words. "Did you enjoy killing?"

Glenn's eyes snap back to his in anger. "No!"

"Did you keep count of each body? Take pride in the number?" He demands not letting up.

"No," Glenn jumps up and begins to pace. "Of course not! It was a job. Kill or be killed. Nothing more."

"After each battle, how did you feel?"

"Relief that I survived. I prayed to God to spare my

life and he did, but sometimes the terror was mixed with exhilaration." Glenn glares at him in defiance. "Does that shock you?"

"Tell me about your last battle?" He demands, ignoring his challenge.

"It was a sea of blood and body parts. My brothers around me were falling. The Cavalry charged first but we... they were prepared for us this time. Trenches were dug..." Glenn sits heavily next to the pastor, "I don't need to close my eyes to relive it. I can still taste the tinge of death. It permeates everything, smoke, blood, urine, and feces but that's not what haunts me."

Glenn is unaware of the tears streaming down his face. "It's the silence after. The moaning, begging, and pleading to God for help. The same God I prayed too." Anger rears and Glenn beats at his chest. "Some of us stayed and gave them what they asked for. It was a mercy compared to the wait others had."

Silence falls for a few minutes while Glenn struggles to compose himself.

"Throughout the Bible, Glenn, war is shown as a dark reality in a damned world. There are vile forces of evil on this earth, and they must be stopped. Sometimes bloodshed is the result. Whether a soldier will be allowed entrance into heaven depends on his own conscious. I don't believe killing in combat is a sin, though it can be. In fact, there are many wars mentioned in the Bible."

"I know that Pastor but-" Glenn stops when Pastor Donegal gets angry.

"No! If you hear nothing else today, hear this! Your entrance into Heaven is not determined by whether you killed during war, but by your faith in a Merciful God. There is no deed big enough to cleanse our souls, we are all born sinners. It is only through God's mercy that we are forgiven. The stones of anger, rage, guilt, and shame are weighing you down. Will you let them bury you, too? Enough men have died. To receive Gods mercy, you must first show yourself mercy."

Glenn hangs his head, "I want to be better, do better. I'm just not sure where to start."

"You just did, son. Recognize that you aren't alone, Glenn, and realize that only God has the right to judge us. Talk to your family. They love you and will understand."

"Will your pray for me, Pastor?" Glenn asks.

"I can do better than that, I can pray with you." Together they walk into the church to pray.

Anika soaks in a hot bath till its tepid then dries off and puts on a riding shirt with the denims she borrowed from Savannah. All cried out she feeds the boys, savoring the way they feel in her arms. If things don't change, hard choices will have to be made, but not today. "That pig is not going to ruin my plans. I'm going to enjoy the rest of my day off with Delaney." She asks the housekeeper to prepare a picnic lunch only to find Delaney sewing with Daisy.

"If it's okay, Mama, I want to stay with Mrs. Daisy."

"Of course, if Mrs. Daisy says it's okay."

"I'd love the company. Are you sure you should be riding?" Daisy asks with a worried glance at Delaney.

"I'm fine. I hope you both can forgive me for yelling at Glenn, but..."

Daisy stands up quickly and steps in front of her. "You said what needed to be said at least you were brave enough to face the beast inside of him."

"Mr. Glenn's not a beast, his heart's just broke.

Mama's gonna fix it, right Mama?"

"Delaney I can't-"

"You have to Mama!" Delaney jumps and runs to grab her hands. "Sometimes his bad dreams keep him up and he's calling for help but no one helps him. You have to save him, Mama."

Daisy covers her mouth with her hand and fights tears, how could they all have been so blind.

Anika stoops down and hugs her daughter tight. "Delaney, I love your heart. It is a beautiful reflection of God's love. I will promise to pray really hard and be a good friend to Glenn, okay, but only God can heal what is broken."

"We can love him really hard and then God will heal his heart?"

"Of course. I'm going to ride to the pond and enjoy the sunshine, do you want to come with me?"

"No, I want to work on my sewing." Delaney skips back to her chair and Daisy wipes her cheek and smiles at Anika.

"You have an amazing daughter."

Pride fills her heart. Anika nods and leaves quickly. She straps on the lunch basket and mounts her hoarse. A smile of exhilaration flickers as she kicks the horse into a trot. Allen watches her leave from the barn and grins when his wife and Delaney walk over.

"Two of my favorite girls," he calls out.

"Where's Glenn?" Daisy asks.

"Checking fences." Allen smiles as Delaney chases a kitten around the yard.

"Anika is riding to the pond, for a picnic. What do we do Glenn? How do we help them?" Daisy frets.

"We don't. Just this once we're going to be still

and let God handle it. He is working on it. We just have to trust." He pulls his wife into his arms and kisses her forehead.

"It's so hard to watch them suffer." She sighs melting into his hug.

"Yep. Now where's my lunch?" Daisy groans and Delaney giggles.

"Your always hungry, Mr. Allen."

"Hungry for little girls," he growls, and Delaney runs screaming with Allen chasing her.

Chapter 28

Anika waits till she is out of sight of the main house and then urges the horse into a run. Images of her childhood in the Virginia mountains roll through her mind. She races across the field, laughing and puts her face up to the sun.

Glenn is riding back to the barn slowly when he hears her laughter. He watches as Anika races across the field in a moment of unabandoned joy and a smile curves his lips. Decision made he kicks his horse into a gallop and follows.

A frown of annoyance flickers when she recognizes the rider coming towards her. She kicks her horse harder, urging her faster attempting to put more distance between them. Glenn watches and gives a kick to his mount who reacts instantly to his rider. Soon, he is riding beside her, waiting patiently for her to realize he's not leaving.

Anika crests a hill and pulls on the reins with a sharp command and stops. She turns to glare at him. Glenn slows and stops before pushing his hat back on his head. His mount stomps the ground, frustrated at the short run.

"That was impressive, I didn't know you could ride

so well."

"My grandparents insisted on lessons when I was Delaney's age." She smooths a nervous hand over her hair and glances away from him. "Well, I'll just be going." When she attempts to move Glenn shifts his horse over.

"Where are you headed?"

"I'm trying to enjoy my day off, Mr. Ward, as instructed."

"Are we back to Mr. Ward? I thought we were friends?" Anika turns away from him and sniffs, struggling to compose herself. In her heart she hears Delaney's words and she sighs.

"I need some time to myself, Glenn. Let me be."

"I can't do that, Anika. We need to talk this out."

"Fine, but not until I finish my ride." Before he knows what's happening, she kicks her mare into a full run, leaving him laughing behind her.

His horse stomps the ground and snorts in frustration, he's ready to run. "Give her a head start, Samson, it's only fair." Glenn leans down and rubs him soothingly, but soon he is as anxious to ride as Samson.

"Ya!" He shouts and leans down low over his mount. Man, and horse ride as one, pounding across the beautiful field. They pass Anika with a whoop of joy. She can't help but slow to watch him and laugh out loud.

Anika trots along realizing she has been duped. "We never stood a chance, girl. That's okay, you did a fine job." She pats her mount, but as she nears the pond her smile fades. Glenn is standing near the water, waiting on her and nerves flutter in her stomach.

"Nice denims," he teases as his hands wrap around her waist to help her down. Anika hisses out in pain. "Damn, what are you thinking riding after..."

"I'm fine. I just need a minute. That pig through me into a table and my ribs are sore." Anika slaps a hand over her mouth when she realizes that she said that in front of him.

Glenn roars with laughter as Anika blushes. "I'm not sorry," she snaps indignantly and tugs on the reins while she waits for him to stop laughing.

"I called him worse, Anika. If it makes you feel any better, he has been taking something stronger than ale and whiskey. I believe they are calling it Black Death because it's a black liquid."

"I could smell it," she whispers, "anyway, I just needed to get out of the house Glenn." She turns to pat the horse munching on fresh grass beside her.

"Just drop the reins they won't go too far. They're well trained." Anika listens before turning to face him. "Where did you learn to ride like that?" She asks, pulling the picnic basket from her saddle. Anika flinches as the weight of the basket sends pain through her shoulder.

Glenn is watching when the pain flashes across her face, he gently takes the basket from her. "I was in the Cavalry unit. It was a requirement."

Anika glances up at him in surprise. Saul spoke often of the Cavalry and the brutality he witnessed gave him nightmares.

"What? Why would you choose that?" She asks.

Glenn laughs a bitter laugh. "Anika we weren't given a choice, you served where they assigned you. Our family were horse breeders, and if could you break a horse and ride, you were Cavalry."

"I see," she murmurs and follows him to the cover of a tree where they could enjoy a picnic.

"You don't see, thankfully, and I pray you never

will." He spreads a blanket from the inside of the basket and she helps him to straighten it before sitting with him.

Anika rubs her shoulder and arm, distracted by the pain that is beginning to make itself known. "Saul was infantry, he didn't speak of it, except after a nightmare."

"I understand. They haunted me for years after I came home, I almost had them beat."

"Almost?" she asks.

"They returned when Sue died," Glenn explains and begins pulling out the food, "I'm starved, what did you bring?"

"I didn't know I would be sharing. Help yourself. I'm not that hungry." Rolls, chicken, fruit and juice in jars and cookies.

"I think she packed plenty for the both of us. I can show some restraint - if I must."

Anika glances up at his playful tone and accepts a plate from him. "Are you sure about that?" She teases as he stuffs a cookie into his mouth and closes his eyes in ecstasy.

"No. I changed my mind. The cookies are all mine." Anika can't help but laugh. Glenn smiles at her, happy to see her relaxing some.

"Tell me about your family, Anika," he urges.

"Not much to tell. They're gone now." She glances at him and sighs. "Mama came to America from Ireland. She was an indentured servant for five years. My father was a banker. They married as soon as she was free to do so. I was their only child."

"How did the daughter of a banker end up penniless?"

Anika is shocked by his forward question, but not ashamed of her past. "Glenn, I was fourteen years old, when Saul began to court me. My Father was not having it. He said the normal things, I was too young. I didn't know what I was getting into. When he refused to give us a dowry, I was hurt and angry." Glancing out over the field she reaches up and pulls her hair free of the band holding it. Her fingers lace through her hair as she combs the tangles out and Glenn's mouth goes dry.

Strawberry blonde waves catch the sunlight and he is sorely tempted to plunge his hands in her hair like his son does. Anika turns to him and smiles. "We were so alike, my Father and I." A breeze lifts her hair. "I see it now. I see him in Delaney."

"She is a fiercely loyal and protective little girl. You've done an amazing job with her," Glenn praises.

"I hope so. She will need to be strong to survive in this world. Could we walk, I'm getting sore sitting here?"

"Of course." Glenn stands, quickly offering her a hand and soon they are strolling in the sunshine near the pond. "What happened with your father?"

"Saul asked me to marry him and he convinced me that my father would come around after we were married." Anika falls silent remembering her mother's sobs as her father refused to see them after the quick ceremony.

"He never forgave me. Mother and I kept in contact through letters. We moved frequently, following the work. Saul worked at the docks in Virginia, until the war started. Delaney was a baby when he joined. He served three years." Her voice fades and she walks towards a large boulder a few feet away. She sits on it, enjoying the wind blowing around her.

"Three years is a long time. I served two years in the Cavalry." Glenn looks down at her and can't help but feel ashamed to stand near her. "I killed so many men like your husband. How can you stand to be around me?"

Anika reaches up to touch him but stops herself. "Did you enjoy it, the killing?" Her question mirrors the pastors.

"No." Glenn shakes his head no before she even finishes the sentence. "I did what had to be done, to survive. Don't get me wrong, Anika, I believed in our cause, still do, but I didn't get a thrill killing from the back of a horse. I would have served until the end of the war if I hadn't been shot."

"How did Sue feel about that?" She asks.

"I didn't care. I was a soldier." Glenn runs a hand through his hair in frustration at her shocked look. "I should clarify that statement."

"Sue and I were childhood friends, members of the same church. Her mother was pushing us to become betrothed, but Sue was more like a sister to me."

"What happened?" Anika asks softly.

"Her mother set up a meeting with our families and arranged for us to be found in a compromising situation."

Surprise ripples across her face. "What?"

"I wasn't stupid, Anika. I knew she had feelings for me, so I avoided her. It was our busy season. Before the war, we had cattle and bred horses. Her father ordered a horse and I delivered it, as I do for any client. Sue's mother invited me inside and told me to wait in the library." Glenn jumps up and starts pacing, anger pushing his steps. His words tumble out, faster and stronger.

"Sue was waiting for me. Apparently, she was in the middle of a dress fitting, minus the dress. She began to cry and threw her arms around me, begging me not go and that's when her parents entered the room. Well, you can imagine the rest. I found myself married to a woman I didn't love, with a family I couldn't trust. I was angry. I enlisted as soon as the war started."

"Glenn I'm so sorry, I had no idea," Anika is stunned.

"I served for two years and only came home because I was shot."

Anika leaps up from the boulder. "Where were you shot?" She is stepping towards him without even realizing what she's doing.

Glenn smiles grimly at her. "It creased my arm, but it could have been much worse. When I came home, it was to a different world. Sue's father had passed away and my parents legacy was in ruins. Anything of value was stripped away. Sue had moved in with my parents before I left. I came home to a very sick wife. The stress of the war took its toll on her and to make matters worse, I found out that Sue was born with a heart problem. She was told early on that she would not live a full life."

"Your saying they knew this before you married." Anika sits back down in complete shock. "How could they do that to you?" She hisses.

"I was livid, but I promised myself when I survived the war that I would try to make a life for us and be a good husband to Sue."

"You can't build a life on lies," Anika says softly.

"True, but Sue's health seemed to rebound with my return. I built our house and we started rebuilding the farm. Dad had decided to concentrate on agriculture while I was away. I'd come to love Sue by then. When I found out she was pregnant, I was thrilled." He smiles at her. "What I didn't know was that Dr. Parker had told Sue not to risk a pregnancy. It would only cause her heart further strain. You know the rest."

Anika glances up at him with a new understanding. "I'm guess we both have a lot of work to do. I seem to attract the wrong kind of men." She wrings her hands together. "I hope you know that I did nothing to encourage Rhemi."

Glenn smiles at her and grips her hand gently. "Men like him don't need a reason Anika. They see a beautiful young woman, unattached and they believe that entitles them to take. He will never touch you again, I promise. No one will ever raise a hand against you again Anika. Not while I draw breath."

"You can't make promises like that, Glenn." He frowns when she backs away from him and pulls her hand from his. "The one thing I need for you to understand is that I won't raise Delaney in a home where she feels threatened. I love your boys, your family, and our life here, but ..."

"Please, don't finish that sentence. I apologized to Delaney. Now if you will let me I would ask your forgiveness. I didn't mean to scare you or Delaney, surely you know I would never raise a hand to either of you."

"I know that in my heart-" Anika glances away from him and takes a deep breath. "But Saul made a vow to love and protect me, he broke that vow more times than I care to admit." Wrapping her arms around herself, she looks back at him. "My heart and my head don't always agree with each other."

"Then we will take it one day at a time, until I have earned your trust."

"I'd like that. I could use a friend, Glenn."

Glenn holds out a hand and sighs with relief when she reaches out and takes his hand. "I can do that." For now, he thinks. Today proved to him that his heart was falling for her.

Anika smiles when he tugs her in for a quick hug. "I spent some time with the Pastor today. He told me to talk to my family about the war. I didn't realize what a heavy weight I carried. He helped me to see that as humans we can't fathom the depth of love our Father has for us. I carry such guilt Anika, guilt I'm sure Saul carried. The guilt of surviving when so many around us fell. War changed us, and I have to learn to accept the changes."

"That's wonderful Glenn. I've been studying my bible and I'm ashamed to admit it, but I forgot that the cross has spoken. Our sins were forgiven before we ever committed them. When Jesus died on the cross for us, his blood broke every shame. That doesn't mean we can sin willfully, it means through faith, when we sin we only have to ask and accept his mercy."

Glenn grins, "That's it, exactly."

She wipes at her tears. "Race you back?" she teases.

"We will take a rain check on that. You are in no condition to race me; besides you don't stand a chance, woman."

"You have a lot to learn about me, cowboy. I never give up."

"I'm counting on it."

Chapter 29

"The Fall fair is important because we will be able to showcase our livestock, grains, fruits, canned goods, vegetables even handicrafts," Daisy explains to Delaney over dinner.

"That's exciting!" Anika exclaims.

"This is the first one since the end of the war. It will be attended by people from all over," Savannah says.

"Even by certain horse breeders, Savannah," Daisy teases.

Glenn glances at his sister but is more interested in Anika's response.

"Mr. Patrick was nice," Anika smiles and nudges her, "You should make sure to seek him out."

"He wasn't interested in me," Savannah replies and glances at her brother to gauge his reaction.

"Boy must be blind not to notice my daughter," Allen teases and sips on his coffee.

"It's odd that he's coming this far for a state fair. Doesn't Kentucky have one of their own?" Daisy asks.

Anika glances at Delaney avoiding Glenn's eyes as she replies. "He said in his letter that he wanted to inspect the livestock."

"Especially the breed mares," Glenn snorts.

Everyone falls silent in shock and Anika glares at him. "Glenn!" Daisy snaps.

"Forgive me." He says biting an apple and chewing it slowly. "I will make sure Dayton sees clearly what is available to him and what isn't."

Anika blushes at his bold statement while Savannah grins with approval.

"Will they have games?" Delaney asks, oblivious to the tension in the room.

"Games?" Glenn grins, "Pie eating contests, apple dunking booths, chicken races..."

Delaney giggles and claps her hands. "Chickens can't race, Mr. Glenn."

"What? Well don't tell Chuck that," Allen teases.

"Chuck's gonna race?" Delaney's eyes grow huge.

Anika smothers a laugh, at the look of excitement on her daughter's face. Chuck is her favorite chicken and she feeds him daily.

"Of course." Glenn stands up and Delaney lifts her arms for him to pick her up. "All the love you gave him made him crazy fast." Delaney wraps a small arm around his neck and cups his clean-shaven face. They have formed a strong bond over the past few weeks. She has taken a liking to rubbing his face and she giggles, stealing his heart. "He might even win a blue ribbon."

"A ribbon!" Delaney whips around and stares at her mother. "Mama did you hear that, I'm gonna win a blue ribbon!"

Anika laughs and stands up. Her heart trembles at the sight of her daughter sitting trustingly in his arms. She stands and moves close to them. "I heard, and I'm entering my Gran's pie in the pie tasting contest."

"We can both get blue ribbons Mama!" Delaney

reaches out and wraps an arm around her shoulder. "Mr. Glenn what are you entering? You have to win too."

"I think I've already won the best prize, Delaney," he murmurs softly.

Anika's heart trembles as she thinks of the change in him. The past few weeks they have started studying their bible together on Sunday evenings. Glenn has taken time to rest and sleep. His appetite has returned, and he has taken to spending time with Delaney. Fall allows them time together and she has decided to trust Gods plan.

"Did you hear that Daisy? Anika is baking. We will clean up you get started so we can test taste for you," Allen orders.

Everyone laughs as Anika walks over to Glenn and plucks Delaney from his arms. "I thought you might say that. We must go to the cellar and see what supplies I will need to make my pie. But you have to promise not to tell anyone the ingredients."

"Why, Mama?"

"It's our secret family recipe." Anika walks through the kitchen and towards the back door unaware that Glenn is following her.

Delaney frowns and pulls her mother's face back to her. "I thought we were all family," her voice hitches as Anika stops walking.

"Oh, Delaney, you must know I was only joking. You can tell anyone you want the recipe."

Glenn listens quietly to see how she will handle this. It occurs to him that Delaney is right. They are family and should be a family. He wants a future with them, now he just has to convince Anika that he is a changed man. With his families blessing he is going to start courting her.

"But Mama, Mrs. Batcher said that we are trash, and that I can't call the Wards my family." Anika jerks as if slapped and sets Delaney on her feet and stoops to her knees.

"Mrs. Batcher and I will talk about that on Sunday. I need you to hear me, we are not trash, Delaney, and the bible speaks very clearly about gossiping. That means talking ugly about someone."

Glenn steps up behind her and speaks clearly, startling her. "In Isaiah 54:17 it says, 'No weapons formed against you shall prosper and every tongue which rises against you in judgement, you shall condemn.'

Stooping down eye level with Delaney he says firmly, "Some families are born together, and some are brought together by our Father, God. We are that kind of family."

Delaney throws her arms around his neck and squeezes tight. "That's what I thought." Anika wipes a tear and takes the hand he offers to pull her to her feet.

"Now, let's go to the root cellar. I don't want you down there alone."

Anika smiles in relief. "Thank you," she says as Delaney wiggles to be put down and runs out the kitchen door with a skip and smile.

"Family supports each other, Anika. I meant what I said to her," Glenn whispers.

Unsure what to think Anika hurries out the door and puts some space between them. The truth is that Delaney isn't the only one to hear nasty rumors. They are everywhere. In town, at the general store, even at church. She had hoped that time would show them to be untrue, but jealousy and envy are strong enemies to fight. Anger ripples through her heart as she watches her daughter play with the dog. Anika pulls her coat tighter around her shoulders and wonders if things will get better or worse.

Chapter 30

Fall Fair

"Mama! Look!" Delaney bounces excitedly beside her on the wagon seat. Daisy and Allen laugh at her.

A parade of horse-drawn carriages fills the grassy grounds. A cool breeze blows through, reminding them of the fall temperatures. Spread out before them are horses being led by owners, fields, wildlife, and weathered barns. Tents are lifted to the sky, providing shelter for the visitors and sellers.

"I wish I'd brought my camera," Savannah sighs.

"I'd forgotten how magical it is. It's like a magical city just arose, and we get to visit for one day!" Anika gasps, glancing out at the massive hundred-acre field set up for the huge crowds they are expecting.

"One day? No, we can't possibly see everything in one day. We have hotel reservations for two days," Daisy says with a grin as Allen lifts her from the parked wagon.

"Two days!" Delaney claps her hands with glee, and Anika laughs. Savannah hands down Quinton to her mother, and Anika hands baby Allen to his grandpa. Glenn lifts down Delaney and helps Anika down.

"Let's go make some memories," Glenn whispers, and Anika pulls away with a small smile.

"This year we are lucky to not enter too many contests. First up are the fruit preserves, bread tasting contest, quilt, and pie tasting contest," Daisy explains.

Allen laughs at the look on Anika's face. "Oh, wait for it. She's just getting started."

"What about Chuck?" Delaney demands. "He needs a

blue ribbon."

Savannah laughs and takes Delaney's hand. "I love your attitude. We most definitely are bringing home a ribbon, dear heart."

Glenn removes the pram from the wagon. "This is a luxury," Anika murmurs as they lay the boys inside.

"Only the best for our boys," Glenn teases.

Anika stares at him in open-mouthed shock. Daisy nudges Allen and grins. "We will take Delaney to check on Chuck and grab a candy apple."

Savannah walks away with Delaney, following Allen and Daisy.

"Glenn?" Anika tucks a blanket around the boys and glances up. "What is going on?"

"Today we are going to relax and be together as a family. I want to make some good memories, win some ribbons, and spoil you and Delaney. Do you trust me?"

The sounds and smells reach her ears, and her heart stutters. "Yes, of course I do."

"Good," he presses a kiss to her forehead and smiles down at her. "Mrs. Henrietta will be at the hotel at one, and Mom and Dad are going to take the boys to her, so we can stay and have fun."

Anika's mouth falls open in surprise. "Glenn! When did you plan that?"

"Mrs. Henrietta was happy to do it, especially when I told her she could ride on the train instead of a wagon. I booked a room for her and the children, so we could relax. It's next to yours." He starts pushing the pram forwards, following the family.

"Glenn, you've thought of everything."

"You have no idea, Anika. I can be downright conniving when I need to be."

"I'll keep that in mind," she replies with a laugh. A squeal of excitement from Delaney draws their attention.

"Hurry, Mama. It's time for Chuck to race!"

The rest of the morning flies by, starting with Chuck winning second place. Delaney grudgingly accepts her yellow ribbon, with a promise from Allen that next year he would win first. She's quickly distracted by a musical minstrel and his dancing monkey.

As they stroll through the fields of tents and stalls, Anika can't help but feel like part of this family. Glenn is attentive and true to his word. Daisy and Savannah purchase various items from bread to preserves, even an oil painting for Savannah's room.

The boys wake up and start fussing; luckily, Anika thought to bring two glass bottles of juice for them. Now that they are stronger, they can handle some watered-down juice in between feedings.

Allen and Glenn wander towards the stalls set up for the livestock to be judged. From chickens, pigs, hogs, and sheep to beautiful race-quality horses. Anika, Daisy, and Savannah take Delaney to see the animals. Anika is laughing at Delaney and the piglets when a familiar voice calls to her.

Dayton Patrick hurries to her side and grabs her hand, pressing a quick kiss to the back of it. He is dressed in denims and a hat with riding boots and looks quite dashing.

"Dayton, it's nice to see you," Anika says, smiling at him. Though surprised at his forwardness, she makes note that his nearness doesn't affect her like Glenn.

"I was hoping to see you. You're in time for the horse race." Dayton keeps her hand for the moment, and she pulls away and looks behind him to Glenn and Allen making their way through the crowd behind him.

"Horse race? Do you have a horse in the race?"

"You could say that?" He grins down at her, "I saved you and Delaney a seat up front."

"Dayton," Glenn says, walking up behind him. "Anika and Delaney will be sitting with my family, where they belong."

Anika bites back a smile and tucks an arm through Glenn's, surprising everyone. "Thank you for thinking of us, Dayton, but Glenn is right. Though we'd love to cheer for you."

Dayton tips his hat back on his dark hair and stares back at them with a grin. "I don't know about that, Anika." His dark eyes tease Glenn, "You didn't tell her you were racing me?"

"What?" All three women say in unison.

Dayton laughs out loud and slaps Glenn on the shoulder, "Good luck, Ward, you'll need it to beat me. Excuse me, ladies." He turns and hurries to his stall.

"Thanks for that, Dayton," Glenn calls to his back. Facing his family, he grins, "We should get you to your seats; I have to check on my horse. Dad will show you the way."

"Follow me," Allen says, pushing the pram and guiding Daisy, Savannah, and Delaney to the makeshift stands.

Anika glares open-mouthed at everyone as they walk away before racing after Glenn. She catches up to him at his stall. "Glenn, you don't have to race him. This is ridiculous."

"Are you worried for me or Dayton?" he demands, pulling her close to his chest.

"Don't be ridiculous, Glenn. He doesn't stand a chance against you," she says, patting his firm chest.

Glenn lifts her chin, "That's right." He kisses her firmly on the mouth and pushes her gently towards the stands. "Now go enjoy the race."

Anika stares at him, "Wait, Glenn," he turns to look at her, and she grabs a fistful of his shirt and pulls him towards her. "I need to give you a good luck kiss." Her hand wraps around the back of his neck, and she tugs him gently towards her. She waits a heartbeat, savoring the manly scent and sharp inhale of his breath before capturing his lips. It begins softly, before gathering heat, causing Glenn to rumble with pleasure. His groan echoes in the stall, and she grins against his mouth, satisfied. She pushes back and snaps, "Now, go win me a blue ribbon."

His laughter follows her from the stall. "Yes, ma'am." Anika joins them at a row of wooden benches and sits next to Savannah and Delaney. "This is a half-mile race, called the Harness race. Don't worry, Glenn has been riding since he was three," Allen explains.

"Yes, but Dayton is racing on Survivor, Allen. He's the fastest horse in all of Kentucky and Virginia," Anika glances at the racers lining up on the grassy field. It is an oval track of sorts, with people and wooden benches forming the barrier.

"Where do you think Survivor came from?" Savannah smiles at the shock on Anika's face.

"Surely you don't mean that he bought her from Glenn?" Anika gasps.

"Not quite." Allen points at Glenn's horse, "His horse, Samson, and Survivor are from the same brood mare."

"I bet five dollars on Glenn," Savannah says, munching on a bag of toasted walnuts. Delaney giggles and sticks her hand in the bag when offered.

"Savannah!" Daisy starts to reprimand her only to be nudged by Allen.

"Tell them, wife," he orders. Daisy sniffs, "I bet ten." They all start laughing at the shock on Anika's face.

"You're all pirates," she says with a smothered grin.

Anika glances around the field and stares in awe at the over four hundred people in attendance. Things are about to get loud. Savannah whispers to Delaney, who quickly covers her ears.

Well-muscled horses line up in the grassy fields. From fillies to stallions, no two are the same and all are striking animals. The twenty animals line up, snorting, stomping the ground, and raring to go. Anika is surprised to see the youngest jockey is just eighteen. Her eyes are drawn to Glenn and Dayton. Both men are striking, but Anika's heart and hands tremble as she watches the change come over Glenn.

One minute he is smiling and relaxed, and the next second, he leans low over Samson and murmurs in his ear. The instant the gun goes off, they erupt in an explosion of energy. Anika watches with her hands clasped together. Her heartbeat matches the rhythm of the pounding hooves, and she can swear the very ground rumbles beneath them from the power of the majestic animals.

In the crush of animals and men, Dayton fights to pull ahead. Some of the riders are in it for the fun, others for the prestige, but most want the three-thousand-dollar purse. Samson is used to riding in a crush of men and animals from his time in the war. It doesn't bother him or his well-trained rider. Not even when a jockey next to him whacks at him with his whip. Glenn is ready for it and grabs the whip, holding it tight and steering Samson closer to the man's horse, causing him to panic. The rider struggles to stay in his saddle with only one arm free to control his horse. Glenn releases him with a shove, and they veer to the side, giving Glenn the opening he has been looking for. He leans forward and yells; Samson reacts instantly with a push of energy.

Anika watches as four horses pull forward, instantly separating themselves from the pack. Glenn leans over, and it seems as if rider and man become one entity. Dayton pulls next to him as they close in on the finish line.

Everyone leaps to their feet, cheering for their favorite rider. Both babies wake up, startled by the noise. They have no clue their daddy is closing in on the best rider on the east coast!

Glenn grins at Dayton and kicks one last time, urging Samson to take the lead. They cross the line with Dayton just pulling ahead of Glenn by a few inches. The rest of the riders thunder across.

Dayton is laughing as Glenn jumps from his mount.

"You had me worried for a second, Ward," he laughs. "I almost had you, Patrick, maybe next year." Samson stomps his feet, and Glenn trots him away to be wiped down as the crowd of people surround Dayton. A blanket of flowers is placed over Survivor's back, and Glenn pats Samson.

"You did good, boy." He spots his family hurrying to meet him and dismounts.

"Well rode, son," Allen says with a whack on his back, and Daisy hugs him. "Thank you." He looks to Anika and asks, "What did you think, Anika?"

"I've never seen anything more magical, Glenn. You and Samson ride like you're one being. It's impressive."

"I agree," Dayton says from behind, surprising everyone. "In fact, I'd like to invite you to race in Kentucky. I'm building a new flat racing track. It's bound to draw prized horses and seasoned riders from end to end of the East coast. Glenn, with a horse like Samson, all you need to do is win some titles, and the purse will be substantial."

"How substantial?" Glenn asks with an interested gleam in his eye.

"First place will receive twenty-five thousand dollars." A collected gasp flickers around the group. Dayton grins, "The fee to enter isn't cheap, but if you win, you can use the money to set up your breeding business again."

Glenn glances at his family, "I'll think about it."

"Don't think too long, Ward. If you'd let a smaller rider on your horse, I wouldn't have stood a chance. Samson is magic. I'll talk to you soon." With a tip of his hat, he leaves, avoiding Anika. It is easy to see she is where she belongs.

A tug on his hand has Glenn stooping down to hear Delaney. She holds up her ribbon and says, "I'll share my ribbon with you."

"Delaney, I don't need a ribbon. You are the best prize." He scoops her up to her delight and giggles, declaring, "I need food. I hear the pie judging is starting soon. Let me put Samson away, and we'll go eat."

Whatever is left of Anika's defenses fall away in that moment. What will she do?

"I love him," she whispers as he sets Delaney on her feet and leads Samson away.

'Trust,' the Lord whispers to her heart.

Heavenly scents waft on the air, as the judges prepare to taste test the pies. Apple, pumpkin, cherry, pecan and walnut, pies so many to eat and so many to taste. Each entrant was asked to bring three pies each for the judges.

"Welcome to our pie judging. We will be judging on three criteria, appearance, taste, and crust. This is a blind tasting, which means we do not know who made which pie, though I'm sure you all know, please try to keep it to yourself."

Anika smiles at the other ladies, standing on the sidelines. Each pie is numbered. Delaney is twisting her hands and looking at her then back at the table.

Anika's pie is called Apple Pecan pie. It was her grandmother's recipe. It is a traditional Pecan pie, but on the bottom of the pie, instead of pouring in chopped pecans, thinly sliced apples are layered with pecans sprinkled on top and topped off with the filling. Then to hide the apples, whole pecans are placed on top to create a beautiful golden top. The secret ingredient is the bourbon. Only a splash but it gives a richness that will make it stand out from the other pies.

Glenn stands behind Anika and bounces one of the boys, nervously watching the first round. When she makes it to round two he grins at Delaney who is beaming with excitement. Round two only has ten pies remaining. The judges drink water between each bite and are somehow able to maintain blank faces as they continue. After a heated debate three pies are chosen for the final round. A pumpkin pie, a cherry pie, and Anika's Apple Pecan pie.

Glenn hands the baby to his mother and steps behind Anika. She reaches back and grips his hand for support. The three pies are judged on appearance first and she thankful that Delaney talked her into adding the piecrust leaves along the edges.

Taste time, each judge is given a healthy slice. They taste, write and taste again. One of the judges takes a fork to the pie and scrapes back the topping on Anika's pie trying to determine what the unusual flavor in the pie is. Delaney hides her face in her mother's skirt and Anika hugs her close. The third test is the crust. Anika's is a flaky pastry crust with a beautiful golden color.

The judges talk and step in front of the table to confer and when they step back one of them holds Anika's pie, with a blue ribbon! Delaney squeals and jumps up and down, while Glenn presses a kiss to her temple.

"That is one of the best pies I've ever had, Mrs.?" The judge asks, shaking her hand.

"Mrs. Coltrane and thank you, but I can't take all the credit. It was my grandmother's recipe passed down from her mother."

The judges pull Anika to the table to have her picture taken with her pie and ribbon while the family watches. Glenn is surprised to find Dayton watching from the back of the tent. He makes his way to Dayton.

"What are you doing here, Patrick?"

"Don't worry, Ward. I can see the way of things. You plan on making an honest woman of her?" He demands.

Does he? When the judge asked for her name it irritated him to hear her give Saul's name. He grins at his friend, "If she'll have me. She could do better, but God brought us into each other's lives and I plan on trusting him."

"Good plan. Walk with me, Glenn."

He follows him outside the tent. Dayton removes his hat and twists it nervously in his hand. "I'm just gonna come right out with it. I took the liberty of having a friend investigate Anika's family." He lifts a hand when Glenn startles.

"Let me finish. I knew her father, and it didn't sit right with me that he left her penniless." Dayton draws a stack of papers out that are folded. He offers it to Glenn. "This is a copy of her Father's will. He left her everything. From the house, land, livestock, and money."

"What? How could she not know this?" Glenn demands taking the papers and opening it.

"They said her husband tried to claim it. He returned all her family's letters, letting her think they abandoned her. When they died he tried to claim the inheritance, but the stipulation was that she and only she, could inherit. The estate has a trustee and now that her husband is dead, it's all hers. Anika isn't penniless and shouldn't be working like she is."

"Why would you do this?" Glenn demands gruffly.

"I had the honor of meeting her father and his legacy should be treated with the respect it deserves. You'll see that she knows about this."

"Of course. Thank you, Dayton," he replies hoarsely.

"Don't thank me, just take care of them."

Glenn watches him walk away and can't help but wonder what this means for them. She will have the means to leave them now and he will have to let her go.

His family comes out of the tent and Delaney waves her blue ribbon, proudly at him. He tucks the papers in his shirt and smiles back.

"We did it, Mr. Glenn. We won first place!"

"Of course, you did, only winners at our house." His eyes meet Anika's and he says, "I'm so proud of you, Anika."

"It's just a pie," she blushes and stammers.

"A blue ribbon pie!" Savannah nudges her and one of the boys begins to cry in earnest now.

"That's our signal. We should be getting back to the hotel," Daisy informs them.

"I'll meet you later, I have to deal with the horses." Glenn hurries away to speak to his mother in private before leaving.

Anika glances back as he walks away as Daisy and Allen talk about the day's events.

"Are you okay?" Savannah asks.

"I guess. Glenn seems so different these past few weeks."

"It's because of you, Anika."

"No," she is quick to say. "That honor belongs to God. He is healing his spirit in ways that I couldn't have."

"True, but you are healing his heart and maybe if you trust, he can heal yours."

Anika tears up at that. "He already has."

Chapter 31

Anika settles into the hotel, marveling at the shared room with Savannah. Mrs. Henrietta and the children occupy the adjoining room, featuring a large picture window overlooking a river and a fireplace with a stone surround. As Mrs. Henriette bathes the twins, Anika tends to Delaney.

"It was a fun day, Mama," Delaney says, stifling a yawn as Anika helps her into her nightgown.

"Yes, it was. I can't believe we won!"

Delaney embraces her, exclaiming, "I like winning."

"Me too, but we won't always win. The joy should be in the experience. It's how we make memories. Don't get caught up in always being the best."

"Okay, Mama."

"Quinton is ready to be dressed," Mrs. Henrietta calls, and Anika promptly assists. Soon, both boys are dressed and asleep with satisfied bellies.

"You go on and get your bath, Ms. Anika, and I will read with Delaney."

"That sounds lovely. Delaney, my room is right through that door, okay?"

"Okay, Mama. Mrs. Henrietta, you should have seen Chuck run. Some of the chickens just pecked the ground, while others ran the wrong way, and one played dead on the ground. Chuck was amazing!"

"I ain't never heard such a thing, chicken races?"

Anika laughs as she enters her room. Savannah, already changed, fixes her hair at a dressing table. A fire flickers, casting a golden glow.

"What's so funny?" Savannah asks, turning with a smile.

"It's Delaney and Chuck. I don't think she'll ever get over him coming in second."

"It was a good memory to give her. I'm going out for a little while. You should take a nap and rest." Savannah leaves before Anika can ask questions.

Frowning, Anika takes a quick bath and changes into a clean dress. Dinner awaits in the downstairs dining room. Just as she finishes her hair, a knock sounds.

"Come in," she calls, turning with a smile to find Daisy at her door.

"You look refreshed," Daisy says.

"I feel better. How about you?"

"I'm going to keep an eye on the children with Mrs. Henrietta. Glenn has asked that you join him for tea in the gardens outside."

"The Gardens?"

"Oh, Allen and I walked through when we first arrived. They have a maze garden with glowing lanterns, walkways, and even seating areas for evening tea."

"That sounds lovely. Thank you." She hugs Daisy and is surprised by the woman's grip.

"Is everything okay, Daisy?"

"Yes, I'm just feeling sentimental. Thanksgiving is coming, and I feel so thankful to have you and Delaney in our lives. You should know how blessed we are that you are here."

Anika sniffs back her tears. "Thank you, Daisy. I can't believe how quickly you all feel like family."

Daisy laughs and pushes her gently to the door. "Go on now before I cry. Take a wrap; it's getting cold."

"Yes, ma'am," she laughs and wraps her navy-blue wrap around her shoulders.

Anika walks quickly out and down the stairs to find Glenn waiting for her. He frowns at her, and her stomach erupts in butterflies. Before she makes it down the last step, he reaches her and rests a hand on her hip.

It is only natural for her hands to rest on his shoulders. "Why so worried, Mr. Ward?" she teases.

"It's nothing," his eyes drop to her mouth, "You look beautiful."

Anika blushes and glances around the empty lobby. "Glenn?" she murmurs.

He steps back, and she follows him down the last step, missing the feel of his touch. "Tea is in the gardens," he offers her his arm and guides her through the lobby and down a hall leading to the back of the small hotel.

Anika gasps when they step outside. Trimmed bushes create a maze of walkways and paths, lit with gas lanterns.

"The sun will be setting in an hour and at night the gardens look enchanting."

Anika glances at him as he begins to chat and give her the history of the gardens. Glenn doesn't do small talk, she thinks. He's nervous. Why is he nervous? Her heartbeat accelerates as they walk, and he seems to be walking quickly now.

Finally, he guides her to an opening in the maze where a gazebo is waiting with tea, fruit, and biscuits set up. She gasps in delight.

"Glenn, this is wonderful!"

"I'm glad you like it," he takes her small hand in his and wonders at the strength in them as he guides her inside. The weight of her Father's will weighs heavily in his pocket and heart.

She pours the tea and offers him a cup while she butters a biscuit. Her caramel eyes watch him nervously toy with his food before she sits her cup down with a snap.

"What's going on? You're making me nervous."

Glenn jumps before laughing softly. "I should've known you'd call me on it." He takes a deep breath and pushes the small plate away.

"I wanted to talk to you in private. Today Dayton surprised me with some news." Glenn draws some papers from his inside jacket pocket and stares at her. "He hired a Pinkerton detective to research your father's estate."

Anika inhales a sharp breath, and her eyes fly open wide before narrowing with fury. "How dare he! Why on earth would he do that?" she jumps up and starts pacing. "Who does he think he is? That is personal."

"Yes, but..." he tries to explain, but she is waving her hands and rambling.

"He had no right! You wait till I see him again..."

Glenn jumps up and grabs her gently by her upper arms, stopping her tirade.

"You will want to hear this, first." Anika goes pale and lets him guide her back to a chair and scoots one next to her before offering her the folded-up documents.

"This is your father's last will and testament." Anika refuses to take them. She crosses her arms protectively over her chest and stares at them. "No. I don't want to know, Glenn."

"Yes, but you need to know." Slowly, he unfolds the papers, placing them on the table beside her. She reaches a trembling hand out and traces her father's script.

"I don't know if I'm strong enough to read it, Glenn. Tell me what it says," she pleads.

"You are the sole surviving heir; he left everything to you and Delaney."

Anika jerks as if slapped, "No! He hated me, Glenn, he refused all my letters." Tears fill her eyes and slip down her cheeks.

"No, he didn't." From his other pocket, he draws out a bundle of letters tied with a brown cord. He places them on the table beside her. "Saul lied to you. Your father's letters were returned unopened."

Glenn was prepared for the fury, anger, rage but not the wail of sorrow that erupts from her soul. It rips from her soul and batters him. She drops her head into her hands and sobs.

"It's going to be okay, Anika," he promises as he lifts her from the chair and into his lap. Her body is wracked with sobs, shaking him to his core.

"I thought... he hated me... Glenn, why would Saul do that to me?"

"I don't know," he answers honestly and hands her a handkerchief. "You need to look at this as a gift," she pushes back and stares at him in shock.

"A gift?" her red-rimmed eyes glare at him, and she leaps to her feet.

Glenn lets her go, glad to see the energy return to her body. Anything but the shattered soul, screaming for help.

"A gift?" her eyes look at the table. "He was

supposed to be my husband, Glenn, not a monster!"

"True. There is no refuting that, Anika, but the facts are that your father and mother loved you. He left you everything, Anika. There is a trustee over the estate, and it is waiting for you. You have a plantation, with horses and livestock, money, and a means to care for yourself and Delaney. You will never be penniless again."

"I don't want it," she says instantly.

"Anika, you are upset right now and not thinking clearly. You are the daughter of a U.S. Senator. You want a way to protect your daughter, and God has given that to you."

"God gave me your family first," she whispers, stepping close to him. "I don't want to leave you."

Relief floods through his body, "Thank God," he jerks her into his arms and hugs her tightly. "Thank you for saying that, but as your friend, I want you to take some time to let this sink in. Read his letters and let it heal your heart."

Tears flow again as she clings to him, "Can we go home?"

"Of course, we'll leave in the morning."

Chapter 32

Anika floats through the next few weeks in a daze, still unable to bring herself to read her father's letters. She contacts the trustee and begins the process to sell everything, except the horses. They will be brought to the farm, and with the money from the sale of the land and property, she will never be short of money again. Her fury at Saul grows with every passing day. What kind of human being takes away everything from someone to cause them pain? She reads her Bible, but the words fall flat. Sleep evades her, and she purposely avoids Glenn, spending time fixing up the homestead. The Thanksgiving service comes, and sitting in church that morning, listening to the words of Pastor Donegal, she wonders how all the people around her can't hear her screaming heart.

"Thanksgiving should not be a response to getting what you desire or think you deserve," the Pastor says, jerking her from her dark thoughts. "Thankfulness should be given in every moment, but you have to purposely seek it. Until you always notice the little things and constantly seek the good even in hostile situations."

"How is that possible?" Anika wonders. "How do I do that?" she asks as Pastor Donegal looks directly at her. "Start by bringing thankfulness to your experiences, instead of waiting for the perfect day or moment. Now, I'm gonna shock some of you when I say this. You don't have to mean it, at first. Where the mind goes, the heart follows."

Anika drops her eyes and glances over to find Glenn staring at her. She looks away and listens intently to the Pastor.

"The Bible says, rejoice always, pray without ceasing, give thanks in all circumstances, for this is the will of God in Jesus Christ for you. Pray with me."

Anika closes her eyes tightly and prays that God will forgive her for being so angry. "Help me let go of the anger and find peace," she prays. Feeling a little better after the service, she goes to the Sunday school where she finds Delaney playing happily in a corner. Mrs. Batcher is speaking to two other moms, and when they see her, they stop speaking. One woman grabs her son and pulls him from the room.

Anger flares quickly, and as Anika walks towards the women, she wonders if she should give thanks for the lesson she is about to deliver to this woman or pray to God that she doesn't just punch her. Her thoughts cause a smile to appear, and she struggles not to laugh out loud.

"Mrs. Batcher, could I have a word with you, please? In private," she asks politely.

"Excuse us, Mrs. Vestule. I'll see you next week." After the woman walks away, Mrs. Batcher begins cleaning up the room, while Anika follows.

"Yes, Delaney told me some ugly things were said in church about us, and I'd like to clear that up."

Mrs. Batcher stops and turns to glare at her, looking her up and down. "Do you really want to do that here, Ms.

Coltrane?"

"Why not here? It was here that you called us trash and hurt my daughter's soul, and it should be here in the house of God that you ask forgiveness," Anika snaps, no longer able to hold her tongue.

"Forgiveness for what? Telling the truth? Perhaps you should have thought of that before you came to our church."

Anika stares at the woman in front of her with pity. Her graying hair is tied into a tight bun, and her pinched lips show exactly what she thinks of her. "I'm sorry you feel that way, Mrs. Batcher, but your dirty thoughts are only a reflection of your own spirit, not mine."

Delaney runs up and grabs her hand as Anika turns to her. "Sweetie, I want you to go find The Wards," her firm words allow no argument.

Delaney runs from the room as the older woman slams down her books. "Why don't you just admit you are nothing better than the woman at the Blue Horse Saloon in town. You just get paid more." Anika steps back in shock.

"That's disgusting." Anika tries to leave only to have the older woman grab her arm in a tight grip.

"How many families will you taint by being here? How many husbands will you tempt with lust? The men are already lining up to have their turn with you." Anika rips her arm away, violently causing the woman to stumble back.

Trembling with rage, she steps close, and it is only the fear in the woman's face that has her stopping. "I've done nothing to be ashamed of, and I thank God every day for bringing me to this family."

Daisy and Allen return with Delaney in time to

hear her tell Mrs. Batcher, "Nothing you can say or do will make me run from this Church or this family. I am here to stay."

She turns to find Daisy grinning at her and Allen staring at her with approval. "Let's go home, ladies," Allen states.

The ride home from church is quiet. Glenn isn't sure what he missed, but things haven't been the same for weeks. After lunch, Savannah goes to work on her photography while Daisy and Allen go check on the horses.

Glenn finds Delaney and Anika on the porch with the boys. "There you are," he says with a smile. He crawls on the floor where the boys are playing on a blanket and tickles their fat bellies.

Delaney watches Glenn carefully with the twins. Her little hands are clutched tightly together, and she holds her breath as if waiting for him to strike. "My Daddy didn't like us. He liked to hurt Mama," Delaney says.

Glenn stares into Delaney's eyes and recognizes a traumatized soul. Her eyes have seen way more than she ever should have, and he prays for the right words to reassure her.

"Your Father was hurting, Delaney." He lays the baby down on a blanket and focuses on Delaney. "I'm not saying what he did was right. It is never okay to strike someone, but I am saying it is okay to love him and forgive him."

"I want to, but I don't think he was sorry, Mr. Glenn, and sometimes when he kicked her, he smiled," she whispers.

Glenn's heart breaks thinking of the gentle woman who has cared for his sons and saved his family. Anika is mortified by Delaney's revelations, but she knows it will eat her little soul up if she doesn't speak of it.

"Delaney, come here," she calls softly. Delaney walks over and is pulled into her mother's lap.

"The Bible says in Revelations, 'He will wipe away every tear from their eyes, and death shall be no more, neither shall there be mourning, nor crying, nor pain, for the former things, have passed away." Anika takes Delaney's hands, "Do you know what that means?"

Delaney shrugs her shoulders, "I think it means, Daddy is forgiven for hurting us."

"That's right, angel. Rosie is in Gods' arms, protected, cherished, and loved. Daddy is forgiven and all the pain that made him angry is washed away. He loved you, Delaney. When you were born he was so happy. You were wanted and loved. Never forget that."

"I'll try, Mama. Can I go play?" Anika nods her head and watches her run off chasing the dogs.

Bowing her head, she wonders if she will ever believe the words she preaches. Glenn picks up Quinton who has started to fuss and sits in the rocker. Anika glances at him, "I'm sorry you had to hear that."

"I'm not. Thank you, I needed to hear that verse today." Anika glances at him in surprise.

"I like the thought that Sue is free from pain and suffering." He leans forward to stare hard at her. "Tell me what the verse means to you."

Anika stands and walks bouncing Allen who has started to fuss. When he calms down she answers him. "It has multiple meanings to me. For my Rosie, it means that she is held in our Father's loving embrace, free of pain and suffering. For Saul, I guess it's the same. The demons that drove him to drink and ... lash out are no more. For me...,

I'm not sure."

Glenn stares at her and smiles, "You're not sure or you're not ready to share that with me yet?"

"I should lay the boys down for their nap." She moves inside quickly so he doesn't see how his words have touched her.

Glenn follows slowly to a downstairs room they've turned into a nursery. He hands his son over, watching as she tucks them in. Anika turns expecting him to be gone but finds him watching her. "I need to check on Delaney." She moves past him quickly and steps out into the autumn air, thankful for the cool breeze. Allen waves when Delaney joins him for her evening pony lesson.

"You'll have to face your feelings sooner or later," Glenn says from behind her.

"Why? It changes nothing." Anika whirls on him. "Why are you pushing me? I'm doing the job you hired me to do, aren't I?" Her emotions are boiling just below the surface, and he has no idea how hard it is to keep her daughter from seeing it. A blush of anger colors her cheeks, and her hands are trembling as she balls them into fists.

"Of course, you are, but your daughter is picking up on your feelings, Anika," he chides softly. "She is afraid to forgive him until you do."

"How, Glenn? I know that I should forgive, and I even understand he was damaged from the war, but it still hurts!" When the first tear spills, she angrily scrubs it away with her fist. "Who gave you the right to judge me?" she glares at him. Part of her is hoping to anger him and push him away.

Glenn snorts, "I'm not judging you, Anika. I want to help you, the way you helped me."

"I didn't ask for your help." Anika storms past him and into the kitchen to wash dishes.

When Glenn follows, she ignores him while she scrubs. "You're right, you didn't ask for my help, but I'm going to give it anyway because that's what friends do."

Turning to him, she laughs, and it is a bitter cold sound, even to her ears. "I don't need any more friends." Glenn goes still and stares hard at her.

"Just what does that mean?" He demands.

"Nothing," but the tears fill her eyes, and she lifts her chin in defiance. "We don't lie to each other, Anika," he chides her softly.

"Things were said about me at church this morning. It would seem a lot of men want to be my 'friend' when you're finished with me." Anika tosses the cloth on the counter.

Glenn is stunned and horrified. "Finished with you?" He grabs her by her upper arms, and she senses an undercurrent of more beneath the surface. "You know better than that."

Shame fills her soul, she bows her head and rests it on his chest. "I'm sorry, Glenn. I do know better. It was a bad day, and I'm angry. I thought by getting away from the bad memories and starting over we would have a fresh start, but it's not to be."

Glenn softens his grip and pulls her close, "I'm sorry, you shouldn't have to experience that kind of condemnation. Who was it?"

"It doesn't matter." Lifting her head, she stares into his eyes, "This morning I realized that I will never be free of the past. The guilt and burden I carry is mine alone. I've written a letter to seek another wet nurse for you, and I mean to mail it tomorrow." She tries to pull away but instead of releasing her, he shakes her.

"You aren't leaving us, Anika Coltrane," he declares loudly. "You told me once that I didn't have to carry it alone. The guilt and burden you speak about were never yours to carry. You did nothing wrong, and God is waiting for you to let it go, and so am I." Slowly he leans in and presses a kiss to her shocked mouth. Glenn tugs her close and growls in frustration, "Please don't make me wait much longer, Anika."

"Glenn!" she gasps. Never has she allowed herself to hope for more with him. "I, I ... don't understand," she stammers.

"Then let me make it clear for you. I love you. I love your gentle nature, your kind spirit, and your heart for God. I want to make you my wife and be a father to your daughter, but not if you are broken. The boys and I deserve a whole woman. I've waited for you, Anika. I've given you the time I thought you deserved out of respect for what you've been through, but I need you. When you are ready to start our lives together, let me know." Glenn releases her and walks quietly out of the house, leaving a stunned woman behind.

Anika sinks to her knees on the kitchen floor, trembling in amazement. 'Glenn loves her?' How did she miss it? 'When your heart is full of shadow, the light can't find a way through,' she hears in her soul. Tears of joy stream down her face, and she laughs out loud.

Savannah calls from the screen door in the kitchen and enters like always. "Anika! Are you hurt?" she rushes over and helps her friend stand up. "What's wrong, speak to me?" She exclaims.

"He loves me?" She whispers. Savannah freezes and stares at her.

"Who loves you?"

"Glenn loves me."

Savannah laughs. "Of course, he loves you. It's about time he told you." Anika stares at her best friend.

"You knew?"

Savannah shrugs her shoulders. "Everyone knows, Anika."

"What?" she gasps. "How could you not tell me? You're supposed to be my best friend!"

"I am your best friend, and that is exactly why I didn't tell you. Some things we must figure out on our own, Anika. The question is, do you love him?" Savannah pushes her long red curls over her shoulder and sits down.

"I don't know, Savannah. How can I trust my feelings again? I thought I loved another, and..."

"And?" she prompts.

Anika turns and glances out the back door to see Delaney riding a pony. Delaney waves excitedly at her mother, and Anika whispers, "And he gave me my greatest treasure."

Savannah smiles with relief. "Exactly. If that horse kicked Delaney, would you blame her or would you blame the horse?" Savannah demands.

"Neither. I would figure out why he acted out and correct the problem."

"Right, but would you demand that she never ride again because she might get hurt?"

Anika grins at Savannah, realizing how foolish she has been. "No, I wouldn't, because we can't live our lives in fear." Anika feels the chords around her heart loosening as she chooses to let the light of love inside, instead of hiding in the shadows.

"Thank you, Savannah!" She throws her arms around her and hugs her.

Glenn is in the barn brushing a horse down when he hears her behind him.

"I keep fighting voices in my head that tell me I'm not good enough to love you." He turns slowly to look at her.

She steps closer. "You say I am worthy, but I'm afraid, Glenn. What if I'm not strong enough? What if I fail you?"

Frustrated, he pulls her close and kisses her softly.

"You could never fail me, Anika. You just must believe that God made you to love me. Believe that we don't have to go through this life alone. We can share our victories just as we have shared our sorrows. Together we can heal. Are you brave enough to love me?"

"You don't understand, Glenn." Her hands grip his shirt. "I've loved you from the first moment." Tears stream down her cheeks. "Your love healed me. It showed me that I'm strong when I feel weak. I believe I was made to love you, Glenn."

Relief flows through his body, and he presses his forehead to hers. "God's mercy is beautiful, and His grace is our greatest gift. Marry me, Anika Coltrane?"

"Yes!" She laughs when he lifts her with a shout of joy and marches from the barn.

"Glenn?"

"You gave me your word. You're mine now, Anika."

Allen and Delaney are on the porch with Daisy, alerted by Savannah when they see them. When Glenn shouts, "She said yes!" Daisy leaps to her feet with a shout of joy. Savannah laughs, and Delaney squeals.

"Time to plan a wedding," Allen says with a laugh.

Chapter 33

Anika walks slowly to the grave of her husband and daughter, crunching the autumn leaves under her boots and denim. The horse stays where she leaves her, giving her privacy. Hopefully, she will be back before anyone knows she's gone. Both stones are covered with leaves, as most things are in the fall season. She kneels and clears each with a gentle hand.

"Hi, baby girl. I miss you. There isn't a day that goes by that I don't think of you. I like to think of all of you together—Saul, your grandparents, and even Sue. Give them my love." She places a stone painted with a beautiful butterfly on it by Delaney.

"Delaney has a new hobby, painting rocks. Well, truthfully, painting anything. She's really good at it," she says with a laugh. "She sends her love."

The second rock is painted for Saul. It has a rainbow on it.

"Saul, Delaney wanted you to have this as a reminder of God's promise to always bring something good out of the storms that we walk through. I need to tell you-" she sniffs and takes a deep breath, swiping a tear away, "tell you that I forgive you. I know you were sick and broken, and I pray that God has healed your heart the way he's healed mine. I want to let go of all the past hurt, and I know it will take time to get there, but I promise to keep saying I forgive you until I mean it with all my soul. I loved you once, and I know I have to let go of the hate and hurt to walk the path God has chosen for me."

"Daddy, if you're listening," she pulls his letters wrapped in twine out and hugs them to her heart. "I've read all of your letters. Thank you for never giving up on me. Whenever I need to hear your voice, I will read one of your letters and think of you with love. Tomorrow I'm getting married." She smiles up at the early morning sunshine. "I love him, and he will be an amazing father and husband. I wish you were here with me, but I know we will all be together again someday. I love you." She cries silently for a little while and blows her nose.

The horse nudges her, and she laughs, reaching up for the reins.

"I know, the time for tears is over." She swings back up into the saddle and rides for home.

Epilogue

Anika smiles at Delaney when the music starts. "Are you ready?" Standing in matching ivory silk bustled dresses, they are a vision of loveliness. Anika's gown is corseted with tiny ivory buttons down the front.

"Yes, Mama."

They chose to be married in church the Saturday before Christmas, with only a few guests present. Dr. Parker and Clara are witnesses, along with Savannah, Allen, and Daisy.

Some of the church members came after the ad Allen and Daisy put in the newspaper announcing the engagement of the daughter of former Senator Thomas Bowden to Glenn Ward.

Anika and Delaney hold hands and step to the end of the aisle between the pews. Glenn's eyes fill with tears as he looks at them. How could one man be so lucky? He holds her eye proudly with his as she walks toward him. Her eyes fill, and she doesn't try to wipe them away. When the pastor starts talking, Anika doesn't hear the words; she is so stunned by her love for Glenn that everything else fades into the background.

"We are gathered here today in the house of God to join this couple in Holy Matrimony. Who gives this woman to this man?"

"I do," Delaney says clearly, causing Anika to jump and look down at her daughter with a grin. Delaney takes her hand and places it in Glenn's and walks to Savannah.

The witnesses chuckle, and the ceremony continues. "The couple has written their own vows."

Glenn squeezes her hands reassuringly and speaks clearly. "I, Glenn Ward, take you Anika Coltrane to be my wife, loving you now and as you grow and develop into all that God intends. I will love you when we are together and when we are apart; when our lives are at peace and when they are in turmoil; when I am proud of you and when I am disappointed in you; in times of rest and in times of work. I will honor your goals and dreams and help you to fulfill them. From the depth of my being, I will seek to be open and honest with you. I say these things believing that God is in the midst of them all."

He slides a gold band on her ring finger. Anika beams up at him. "Glenn today I choose you to be my husband. I promise to be faithful, honest, and supportive as God watches over us. With God's help, I will be the wife you need, deserve and have chosen."

She slides a matching gold band on his finger. Then she surprises everyone by her next words. "You have shown me a world I'd forgotten. You have accepted me into your heart as flawed as I may be. All I ask of you is to accept me for who I am and who I will become. Accept my heart and cherish it, for it is yours. Love me as I love you. Accept me into your children's lives and let me love them as my own."

Glenn cups her face in his hands. "I will."

"Now, wait a minute, I didn't ask the question yet?" Pastor Donegal chuckles with the family and witnesses.

"Do you, Glenn Ward, take Anika Coltrane to be your lawfully wedded wife?"

"I do."

"Do you, Anika Coltrane, take Glenn Ward to be your lawfully wedded husband?"

"I do."

"Good. With the power invested in me by the State of Pennsylvania, I proclaim you husband and wife. You may kiss the bride."

Cheers erupt, and Glenn draws her slowly in. He kisses her reverently and wipes her tears with his thumbs. "No more tears, wife." He commands.

"Kiss me again, husband," she orders.

Glenn kisses her firmly, and Delaney laughs, jumping up and down.

The End

Thank you for reading my award winning
book, Mercy's Promise.
Fall in love with the Ward family as they discover
the healing power of family, the resilience of
the human spirit, and the profound joy that
comes from embracing love in every season. This
heartfelt novel is a celebration of life, love, and
the enduring bonds that tie us all together.

Read Book 2 Now!

Wild Promise

Read Book 3
Available Now!

Are you a Dreamer yet?

Welcome to the world of The Rivers Brothers, a gripping series by Lynn Landes, set amidst the sweeping landscapes of Wyoming. Prepare to be swept away as you follow the compelling lives of five brothers who run the illustrious Rivers Ranch, a legacy passed down through generations.

Enter the lives of the remarkable women who find their way into the hearts of these rugged ranchers. Strong-willed, resilient, and full of passion, these captivating women prove to be the perfect match for the Rivers Brothers, igniting sparks that will forever change their lives.

Amidst the backdrop of the majestic Wyoming wilderness, witness love, laughter, heartache, and triumph as the Rivers Brothers and their equally extraordinary partners embark on a journey of self-discovery, family bonds, and unforgettable romance.

Get the Series here!
All are available with Kindle Unlimited!

<u>The Rivers Brothers</u>

Lynn Landes
Best Selling Author

What to read next?

I hope you enjoyed this book and want to read more! But where to begin? I have over thirty books to choose from!

Craving stories about cowboys and strong families with a bit of grit? Check out The Rivers Brothers Series!

Need a series about strong women and the men who come to love them? Check out The Women's Work Exchange Series!

Love small town romance with a touch of suspense? Delve into the Questioning Hearts Series!

Tap here to find a complete list of all of Lynn's Books.

xo, *Lynn*

Get Free Books

Do you love western romance with a little suspense? Join Lynn's monthly newsletter to stay updated on what's happening in my world and get a free copy of "A Question of the Heart," *the first installment of the Questioning Hearts Series.*

Can the blacksmith win the heart of the town baker?

More books by Lynn Landes

The Promise Series

Mercy's Promise
Savannah's Promise
Wild Promise
The Promise Series Boxset

Tiny Matchmakers

Love Letters and Lollipops
Silver Charms and the Marshal's Arms
Honeyed Hearts and Prairie Promises
Love in Stitches and the Farmer's Wishes
Pumpkin Spice Wishes and Harvest Kisses
Snowflake Kisses and Yuletide Wishes

The Women's Work Exchange Series

Saving Taylor
Saving Wren
Saving Grace
Saving Danielle
Saving Elizabeth

Questioning Hearts Series

A Question of the Heart (Prequel)
A Question of Faith
A Question of Hope

A Taste of Heaven
A Question of Time
A Question of Honor

The Rivers Brothers Series

Dane's Dream (Novella)
Dust and Dreams
Stolen Dreams
Treasure Dreams
Pierced Dreams
Forgotten Dreams

Contemporary

In Time for Christmas
Mark of Steel
Tis the Season

The Christmas Series

A Wish for Christmas
A Promise for Christmas

The Thief Series

The Marshall and the Thief
The Pirate and the Thief

Stand Alone Books

Perilous Dreams
Will of Steel
A Mouse for the Duke

Best Selling Author

Lynn, a Bestselling Author, writes mystery and romantic suspense and historic romance novels that are clean with underlying messages of faith. Her book "Mercy's Promise" won the Illumination Award for shining a light on Christian Fiction.

Lynn currently lives in the Shenandoah Mountains of Virginia with her husband and three children and six animals. She has more than thirty books published with more in the works- including two children's books.

If you'd like to receive updates via email about book releases, special events, and other happenings please followlynnsthread@gmail.com.

Made in the USA
Middletown, DE
22 December 2024

67919486R00149